I0573361

A Dying Fall

The Shakespeare Murders, Vol. 2

John Paulits

A Wings ePress, Inc.
Cozy Mystery

Wings ePress, Inc.

Copy Edited by: Jeanne Smith
Executive Editor: Jeanne Smith
Cover Artist: Trisha FitzGerald-Jung
Image from Pixabay
Image: depositphotos 40768113 s

Wings ePress Books
www.wingsepress.com

Copyright © 2021 by: John Paulits
ISBN-13: 978-1-61309-537-9

Published In the United States Of America

Wings ePress Inc.
3000 N. Rock Road
Newton, KS 67114

What They Are Saying About

A Dying Fall

Mark Louis just feels as if there is something missing in his life. He lacks direction. He's an actor and an author, and he helped solve a murder several months ago. But still, he doesn't feel focused. He confides this malaise to his girlfriend, Kristy, as the small AWB Theatre Company heads to the tropical island of Illyria at the request of Mr. Barset, who is trying to turn the island into a paradise resort. The company is to perform some Shakespeare to help woo investors. But as soon as they arrive on the island, they are caught up in several murders. Mark is no longer lacking direction.

This is an exciting mystery which Mark has to solve long-distance as the theatre company stays on Illyria for only a few days. Mark comes up with various explanations which his friends find very far-fetched, something a writer might think up. But Mark never gives up, and eventually, with some help from Kristy, he solves the case.

This is the second novel in this series and I feel it is even stronger than the first. The characters are fairly well developed and the plot has a number of twists and turns. The island of Illyria seemed very real and a trifle sad, as it was supposed to be. I loved all the Shakespeare quotes and I agree with Mark that the Bard has a quote for any situation. The clever ways *Twelfth Night* contributed to the plot just increased my enjoyment of the novel.

Mystery lovers, especially those who are also fans of Shakespeare, will certainly enjoy *A Dying Fall*.

—*Long and Short Reviews*

Dedication

To
Joe Meredith and his jet plane
***

One

Early morning. The sky a sparkling blue. The calm and gentle rolling ocean added its azure to the day. The soft greenery of the island caught the day's golden sunlight, and before long, the dappled gray shade would be a much sought-after refuge from the eternal summer's heat.

A squatter, grimier than most, shuffled along the tree-lined dirt road. A bicycle rolled by him, but he ignored it, staring instead at a woman, another squatter, bucket in each hand, who approached along the road, heading for the nearby spring. She would be the one.

The woman approached a triangle of golden light filtering through the trees. As she stepped into the light, the man moved to her side of the road. She looked his way and smiled. The smile startled the man. He paused and the woman passed back into shadow. His surprise had allowed the woman to pass by unharmed, and it angered him. He continued to walk, looking for the next one.

Another bicycle, this one coming toward him, roiled up the dust of the road, and he averted his face. When he turned back, he spotted another woman approaching. She carried nothing, perhaps heading to the marketplace for some early shopping. He kept his eyes averted until she was steps away. He surveyed the road and determined they were alone. He pulled out the sharp, gleaming butcher knife he'd brought with him from home and pressed it against his right leg. The woman came even with him, and as she stepped past, he threw his left arm around her, pulling her head back and exposing her brown neck. He drew the knife across her flesh. Blood spurted, and the woman crumpled. The man looked up and down the empty road. With a swing of his leg, he pushed the woman's body over the edge of the dirt road. It rolled down the hill until it stopped, its legs entangled in undergrowth. He hurried away, surprised how easy it had been.

Two

Malvolio: I'll be revenged on the whole pack of you!

Malvolio, black of adornment, black of mood, stormed from the stage, leaving behind a chortling entourage of unsympathetic associates. Only the duke and his former love, Olivia, showed the slightest of condescending sympathy.

Olivia: He hath been most notoriously abus'd.

Duke: Pursue him and entreat him to a peace.

No one bothered to pursue or entreat him, however, and the actors exited, leaving only the clown behind to toss a few merry sentiments into the air and assure the audience all was one and life a merry game.

After changing into street clothes, Mark Louis—actor, writer, and resident crime-solver—joined fellow troupe members Don Lovett, Kristy King, and Karen Christenson at a table in Phebe's Bar and Restaurant, the local actors' hangout, near the fireplace, flaming cheerily on this mid-January evening. He and his fellow actors basked in the satisfaction of having the play locked a good two weeks before its scheduled opening.

"Have we heard yet?" asked Karen, the most blonde and buxom of his group. "I would dearly love a few days in the sun before we get serious about Shakespeare."

"Me, too," agreed Kristy, who sported a darker, more exotic look. Both women were in their mid-twenties. "Are we going or not?"

"From what Ashley told me, we're as good as invited," said Mark. "This guy, Barset, knows her from when she was married to the late Mr. Brunner."

"Yes, and Ashley said..." Kristy urged.

"They met at one of the parties she's always attending. They got to talking, and he'd like to put on a fancy show to impress some people he wants to invest in his island."

"I don't believe it's really called Illyria," said Karen.

Mark shrugged. "That's what it's called, at least for now."

"I looked for it on a map," said Kristy. "Not there."

"Too small to be noted, according to Ashley," said Mark. "Insignificant and uncivilized, inhabited by squatters only, I'm told. There's nothing there but Barset's fancy estate."

"And Mr. Barset wants to turn it into a resort?" Don asked. He was the main actor of the troupe, the sole member who had an agent looking for better things for him.

"He does." Mark waved the waiter away. "We'll wait for Ashley to get here. Anyway, Barset owns a lot of the island. He has permission from St. Thomas to develop it, but he needs money, so he's treating possible investors to a few days there to look around. Our job will be to entertain them with a classy collage of Shakespeare."

"Well, if we can't get people interested in an island named Illyria by doing a play about an island named Illyria, we should pack it in," said Karen.

"Where will we stay?" asked Kristy.

"In Barset's big house on the island. We'd only be taking the full-time members of the troupe."

"Not Marty?" asked Don. Marty was Marty Schonbaum, a retired English professor who happily participated in all things theatrical.

"Oh, yes, Marty, too. We can't leave our director behind. That should give us enough personnel to do a few potent scenes."

"Ashley's here," said Don. Mark looked over his shoulder. Phebe's always buzzed when Ashley Warrington Brunner arrived. The waiters responded by pulling together a number of tables, and the members of the AWB Theatre Company left their seats to join their patron. Ashley loved having a theatre company of her own. The company had originally been the suggestion of her late, deceased lover, Lawrence, and Ashley, former actress and current theatre devotee, had agreed right off. The company managed to get *Desire Under the Elms* produced before tragedy struck. Ashley caught Lawrence cheating with Karen, but he was murdered the night of his exposure. Mark managed to snare the killer, and Ashley, at Mark's petition, forgave Karen for her indiscretion. The troupe, forced to abandon their run of *Hamlet*, had hung together through its travail and now, having had more than their share of tragedy, looked forward to putting on a comedy, *Twelfth Night*.

Ashley stood at the head of the table. Not quite sixty years old, thin, rich and with long, flowing white hair, she enjoyed basking in the limelight. Her generosity to her actors was well known. "I'm here to give you the good news." She paused and smiled. "We have our invitation."

A cheer arose, even from the temporary members, who would not be making the trip.

"We'll be leaving next Monday and returning on Friday. Everyone will, of course, be paid for the week."

"We'll go back into rehearsal the following Saturday. Okay with you, Marty?"

Marty, too busy smiling to speak, made an okay sign.

"We'll rehearse Saturday through Tuesday, rest on Wednesday, and open on Thursday."

Ashley then went through the details of the upcoming trip.

When the night ended around ten, Don and Karen headed for the subway, arm in arm. They were on-again-off-again lovers, who lived five minutes from each other in Park Slope, Brooklyn. They had tried living together once and failed, but had been getting along so well recently they both believed their relationship could prosper the second time around. Karen, however, insisted they continue to live apart. Less pressure, she said.

"There go the lovers," said Kristy.

"No," Mark said, smiling, "the lovers are right here. Coming home with me tonight?"

"Yes." Kristy entwined her arm about Mark's. "I hate your apartment, but I love you."

Mark lived in a shoddy one-room apartment on Avenue B. "After this evening's happy news, it seems like a nice night to celebrate."

Mark sighed. "I took up with the right woman when I took up with you."

"Let's get home," said Kristy.

Three

The island of Illyria—perfect blue sky, silent ocean breezes, each day sweet and lovely.

A squatter, his heart beating madly, leaned against a tree on the edge of the market clearing. Some two dozen open-air stands sold produce, domestic handicrafts, anything the squatters could come up with to earn their daily bread. A handful of enterprising souls from other islands had built stalls to sell items impossible to manufacture by the squatters. These enterprising souls also took back with them Illyrian items of possible interest to tourists on the bigger islands to be resold at an exorbitant markup and at no benefit to their producers.

People came to the marketplace, and people left. The tense squatter who lounged by the tree studied the people leaving. Finished with their marketing, people started down one of the island's dirt paths toward whatever dilapidated home they had constructed. The squatter looked for someone making the trip alone.

A woman passed by him with a young child in tow. He rejected them and turned back to the market. Another woman, laden with two packages, one in her hand and the other balanced on her head, started onto a path a short way off. He pushed himself away from the tree and stepped briskly across the marketplace toward the same road. He sweated in the intense heat, but his nerves would have caused him to sweat in any weather. He glanced back often, and when the woman disappeared around a lazy curve in the road, he pulled the butcher knife from beneath his shirt, pressed it tightly against his left leg, and hurried forward.

The woman gasped when the strong arm pulled her head back. The long, sharp blade slid from right to left across her neck. Grimacing, the killer dragged the body into the brush and tossed the packages in alongside her. He returned his pace to an island shuffle and continued down the hot, dry road, not allowing himself to look back even once.

Four

The small, single-engine plane banked slightly, enough to give the passengers sitting by the portside window a view of the entire island.

"It looks beautiful," Kristy gushed.

Karen, sitting behind Kristy, quoted, "What country, friends, is this?"

"This is Illyria, lady," replied Don.

"And what should I do in Illyria?"

"Oh, how about swim a little, snorkel a little, party a little, perform a little. You know, the usual," said Don.

"Sounds good," Karen said with a laugh.

Kristy leaned her head on Mark's shoulder and spoke softly. "We'll be on the ground in a few minutes. You haven't said an awful lot the whole flight. You okay?"

"I'm fine."

"Then why so quiet?"

Mark lifted his hand slightly. "Thinking about my life is all."

Kristy arched her eyebrows. "Rather ponderous. What's the problem? Not me, I hope."

"Definitely not you, sweetie. I consider you more solution than problem." He took her hand. "But the acting, the little writing, everything I do. I don't know. 'Enough, no more; 'Tis not so sweet now as it was before.'"

"My, oh my, you've got it bad. We better talk when we get a chance. I had no idea you were so riddled with discontent."

"No, no. Not discontent, but riddled with something."

"We'll figure it out. Put your seat belt on. I promise you we'll figure it out."

Mark smiled at her. "I'll count on that."

"Have you ever met this Mr. Barset?" Don asked from the seat behind.

Mark turned slightly. "I have not. Like I told you, he knew Ashley's husband long ago. She met him again recently at some function, and they've chatted once in a while since then."

"Are they amorously involved?" asked Karen.

"I think not," said Mark. "But Ashley…you never know."

The twelve-seat plane skipped once on the runway a half-mile from the Barset estate and rolled to a quiet stop. As they disembarked, Karen said, "Oh, this heat felt good for the short time we were in St. Thomas. It feels even better now, knowing it's going to last for five glorious days. Are we the last to arrive?"

The pilot, an island native named Carlos, began transferring their luggage from the plane to one of two jeeps meeting them.

"Ashley flew over yesterday," said Mark. "The fancy business meetings have been going on since Friday, I think. The investors'll be here for a full week. Everyone leaves Friday."

Kristy untied her ponytail and shook her black hair free in the island breeze. "Do we know what we're doing yet?"

"You mean on stage?" asked Mark.

"We know perfectly well what we'll be doing off the stage. Don't we, Karen?"

Mark waited for the two young women to stop giggling. "Yes, well, Ashley suggested some scenes from *Hamlet* on Wednesday and *Twelfth Night* on Thursday. It shouldn't be difficult, since we know the lines already. The rest of the time is ours."

Karen spun in a slow circle for a panoramic view. "I wonder whether we can inspect some of the island before we go to the house. I'll go and ask." She walked toward the two drivers who leaned on the nearer of the two jeeps.

"Ashley was right when she said this was a beautiful but desolate place," said Kristy. "Did anyone see the house when we were coming in? I didn't see anything but trees and beach. I hope there's a beach near the house."

"Must be," said Don. "And we'll be on it before too long."

Karen returned. "We can go in the first car. Otavio will take us around. He said the only thing to see aside from Barset's house and grounds is the marketplace where the 'squatters,' he called them, do business. Squatters." She shrugged.

Mark explained. "Ashley mentioned them to me. People from other islands...St. Thomas, who knows where? They somehow end up here when they have nowhere else to go. They throw together a shack and live the best they can. It shouldn't take too much to live here." He looked around. "A little food, a little water—what else would you need?"

"You say that with some longing," said Kristy.

He laughed. "We'll talk, remember? Here come Tony and Marty. Want to drive around the island a little before we go to the house?"

"No, thank you," Marty answered. "Little planes are nice...to disembark from. I've had it for a while. The house, some lunch, a nap. I'll see you there."

"I'll go with Marty," said Tony. "What's to see? This is the most godforsaken place in the world. I had no idea it would be like this."

"Oh, Tony," Karen teased. "You know it's beautiful."

"New York is beautiful. Phebe's is beautiful. This is stagnation, pure and total."

"We're going to cruise the island, anyway," said Don. "Meet you back at the house when we're through."

"If you're going out to see all there is to see, you might beat us back to the house," said Tony.

"I doubt it," Karen said, stepping into the jeep. "You'll be sorry when you find out what you missed."

"Another in a long line of life's regrets. I'll deal with it."

The troupe divided and went their separate ways.

~ * ~

The jeep soon halted on the edge of a crowd milling about the stalls of the marketplace. "This is some scraggly bunch of merchants," said Mark. He and the others left the jeep and walked among the stalls. "Look how they live."

Many shacks ringed the immediate area, and like the spokes of a frail wheel, a few dirt roads led off in various directions from the marketplace.

"This really is subsistence living," said Don. "It might be harder than you imagined making ends meet here. Ladies, would you like to get some food?"

Kristy and Karen agreed, so Otavio led them to a stall and ordered for everyone.

Don glanced suspiciously into his wooden bowl. "What are we eating?"

"Fish and vegetable chowder," said Otavio.

Karen looked around "Where do we eat it?"

"Just hunker down next to a tree, I suppose," said Mark. They followed Otavio to the edge of the clearing and settled onto a small, cool patch of shady grass. One of the dirt roads ran nearby.

Karen swallowed her first spoonful. "What do you think, Kristy? How's it taste?"

"No complaints from me. I like it."

As Mark ate, he studied the scene before him. "We really stand out in this crowd. Three pale blondes and a dark woman of mystery."

"Me?" Kristy said, adding a coy smile. "Mystery?"

"Yes, you." Mark had tried to pluck Kristy's secret from her—background, parentage, and history—but so far had received only love and affection, not information, in return.

After finishing the chowder, they roamed the different stalls. Kristy and Karen each bought wide-brimmed straw hats. Mark and Don, though urged by the vendors, bought nothing.

After adjusting her new hat, Karen said, "I want to get to the beach today."

"I've seen enough, too," Don agreed. "Where's Otavio?" They stopped and looked around.

"There." Mark pointed across the market clearing where Otavio spoke in some agitation with three stall owners. "He's waving for us. Let's go see what's up."

Otavio drew the group aside and spoke in a lilting West Indian patois. "There has been another murder."

"What do you mean 'another'?" asked Mark.

"The third in the past three weeks."

"Who was murdered?"

"A squatter again. A bicycler just found the body lying up the road over there."

Karen gasped. "The road where we were sitting?"

"Does the island have a police force?" asked Kristy.

"No, just Carlos, Haniel, and me. We are security for Mr. Barset. I must inform Mr. Barset of the murder right away."

"How? Can we call?" asked Mark.

"We have no cell service, and the only phone on the island is the one at the house. We will have to go."

They walked back to their jeep, climbed in, and sped off down the road toward Anthony Barset's estate.

~ * ~

"This is outrageous. And at a time like this. Do you realize who I have here now? Right upstairs?"

"I can imagine, Anthony," Ashley said, sipping from a glass of white wine.

Anthony Barset's obvious outrage made Mark uncomfortable. He chose to study the room rather than intrude on Barset and Ashley. "Nice, eh?" he whispered to Don, nodding toward the sliding doors facing the ocean, now open to reveal a long, white beach outside. The sun glittered off the ocean beyond. The room itself was furnished with rattan furniture, and the chairs had deep green, flowered upholstery.

"Very."

"Ashley beckons. I think she wants us to meet her friend."

Ashley stood near the open doors, her long white hair moving in the sea breeze. She rested her wine on a round, glass-topped table and introduced Mark and Don to Anthony Barset.

"My pleasure, my pleasure." Barset shook both outstretched hands vigorously, and Mark logged his first impression of the man.

Anthony Barset looked about sixty and was so oversized it seemed that every visible part of him had been pumped full of air. He had stubby and sausage-like fingers, protruding lips, ragged, unkempt eyebrows and thick, swept-back, oily black hair. A Hawaiian shirt with an impossible conglomeration of colors and baggy khaki shorts did little to improve his appearance. Rolls of fat in his overblown sandal-clad feet quivered as he paced the room.

"Have a drink. Have a drink," Barset insisted.

"Where are Karen and Kristy?" asked Ashley. "Tony and Martin are napping. I don't think they like the beach."

"They're changing into bathing suits," said Mark. "I didn't realize the beach was this handy until we got back to the house."

"Do you know what's happened?" asked Barset.

Mark took a vodka tonic Don made for him. "Only that we were walking around the marketplace when we heard about the murder."

"The third murder in less than a month. I was in New York when I heard about the second one and now another. Only a handful of people on this island, and they wait until I gather the richest investors I can find to start killing each other. It's monstrous. Who the hell's going to invest in a place where people are getting murdered right and left?"

"What can be done about it?" asked Ashley.

"I have three security men on the island. They're security for this house and these grounds. They're not trained to track down murderers. What the hell is going on here? Where's my drink? Make me a drink!" He directed his request to a dark-skinned man in sandals, a white shirt, and white slacks, who stood at the side and now, on cue, moved to the bar.

"Why would anyone kill anyone else on this island?" Barset went on. "The people who got killed were dirt-poor squatters. They own nothing. No one owns anything on this island but me. What's to be gained from killing them?"

Mark sipped his drink. "Maybe someone simply enjoys killing."

Barset stopped pacing and turned toward Mark.

"I've told you about Mark," said Ashley. The breeze had stopped momentarily, and she took a paper fan from the table and waved it discreetly in front of her face. "He identified the man who killed Lawrence."

"Ah, yes. Sad business." He turned again to Mark. "Can you do it again? Can you find out who's doing this and put a stop to it?"

Before Mark answered, Don interrupted, "I'll go find out what's up with the ladies and meet you on the beach, Mark."

Barset put his hand on Don's shoulder. "Yes, yes, do that, Ron. Enjoy yourself. We'll meet again at dinner and afterwards, talk about the performance. Ah!" He took a frosty glass from the servant, and Don made his escape.

"Now, Mark, can you do it again? Can you find out who's committing these murders?"

Mark, grateful for Don's earlier interruption, still had no answer for Barset.

"I know nothing about your island, Mr. Barset, nothing about the people, nothing about the three murders."

"We have reports. We filed reports with St. Thomas. They don't give a shit, though. You can read them. But no one is interested in the island. That's its charm. That's its value. But that's why no one gives a damn about what's going on here. Of course, that's why I was able to buy such a substantial piece of the island, too." He frowned at his glass. "I should have bought the whole damn place. Until we get some development here, until some money's at stake, no one's going to give a good goddamn. If I can't assure my fellow investors, who are right now getting themselves together upstairs for a pleasant cocktail hour and tour of the island, that this is a safe place worthy of a top resort capable of luring money-spending vacationers...ha! Well, this island might as well sink into the ocean. Imagine it. Once here, there's nowhere else to go. People who vacation here will *have* to spend their money on whatever we throw in front of them. We'll organize this tropical paradise as no tropical paradise has ever been organized. Damn, it's a worthy project." Barset drained his glass.

Mark took the liberty of indicating his own empty glass to the white-clad servant.

"I would consider it a great favor, Mark," said Ashley, "if you tried to do for Anthony what you did for me."

"Of course. I'll do whatever I can, but I don't see how we're going to be able to get a handle on what seem to be random killings in the few days we'll be here."

"I'm sure you'll try, Mark," said Barset. "And I'll make it worth your while. You bet I will, but I have to go now." A young native woman had appeared at the door to the room and motioned to Barset. "I'll extend the cocktail hour. This is no time to take them around the island sober. Until dinner then. Enjoy the rest of the afternoon."

Barset left the room and closed the door behind him with a decided slam.

"Will you be needing me?" asked the male servant.

Ashley turned. "What is your name?"

"Adiba."

"No, Adiba. You can go."

The door closed quietly behind Adiba.

"The servant dresses classier than the master." Mark sipped his drink. "This Barset is something. How long did you say you've known him?"

"He worked along with Wellington before Well and I were married. He's a bit younger than my late husband, but you can see the kind of a go-getter he is. They were investment partners, but they went their separate ways soon after Well and I married. After that, we only saw him at the occasional party and soon, not at all. I don't know what happened to him, but he's clearly done well for himself."

"Clearly. So he wants to build a resort on this island and needs money from the people he's gathered?"

"And from me. I'm interested in this project, too, but the money he needs is far above my level. When we met again last month, he told me about this island. He made it sound so attractive. I can only see myself contributing a few million. But the way he described it, I wish I had more courage to plunge. Imagine, a suite in the new resort always available for me. Not a bad place to spend the winter months while making money at the same time."

"Count me in for a hundred or two," said Mark.

Ashley chuckled. "Anthony is right. The murder of these people will be most off-putting for the investors."

"And the squatters, too, no doubt. I'll read the reports and look around, Ashley, but I don't see what I can do in such a short time."

"Anthony will appreciate it. So will I." She turned her head toward the open doorway. "Look how beautiful it is—unspoiled, natural." She looked at Mark. "But deadly. Who knows if even we're safe?"

"Oh, I'm sure we'll be safe enough if we stay close to home."

"Yes, I suppose. Well, why don't you join your friends on the beach? I must get ready for the cocktail hour. Can't have sober investors, you know."

Mark went up to his room and changed into his bathing suit. When he arrived at the beach, Don sat alone in the shade of the wide fronds of a tall tree.

Don looked up at the tropical sun. "*Phew*. Hot."

Mark slumped down next to him. "Where are the girls, Ron?"

"Ron, yeah, I made a big impression on him. Forget it. The girls are here. You should see them. They're in the water."

"Oh, yes, I see them now."

"No, you don't. Kristy is wearing a bathing suit the bottom of which is about one inch wider than a thong would be."

"Sort of a son of thong?"

"Exactly. Karen's suit is a bit more full-bottomed, but, of course, Karen herself is a bit full-bottomed. To compensate, though, she is pouring out of the top of her suit."

Mark let a handful of sand slide from his fist. "When did you become this fashion conscious? Boy, it *is* hot."

"A guy'd have to be unconscious not to notice. Hollywood starlets dress like that, don't they? Something I could get used to. Almost makes me forget I'm going out to Hollywood to act, if I go out at all. I passed a sweet, young native girl when I left your meeting with the great Mr. Barset."

"He is something, isn't he?"

"He nothing. Did you see her?"

Mark stood. "Yes. She came to get Barset. I saw her."

"Gorgeous?" said Don, getting to his feet as well.

"Very. Karen will be thrilled."

"Hey, she's made it clear our relationship is wonderful but casual. Casually intense, she describes it. We still have our own apartments. We've not formally committed to each other. We tried once before, and it didn't work well, remember? She won't have it."

"I remember. My shoulder hasn't dried out yet from you crying on it."

"Well, it's her idea to be uncommitted lovers. I can at least look, can't I?"

Mark returned Kristy's wave. "If you say so, but you do realize what women say and what they mean are often unrelated."

"Yeah, yeah, I know, but the native girl was gorgeous—so creamy brown."

"Kristy looks a shade Asian, don't you think?"

"Is she?"

"Asian?"

"Asian."

Mark shrugged. "I can't find out. She won't tell me anything about her past or her family, but her hair, her eyes, her complexion. I'll figure it out."

"I'm sure you will. The girls are calling us. Let's go in the water. And be forewarned. Our two sea nymphs are almost wearing bathing suits."

Mark laughed. "Once more unto the...beach, my friend."

Karen and Kristy ran to the water's edge to welcome the two men.

Kristy threw her arms around Mark. "This is so great."

"Yo, cold!" he yelped, stepping back.

"Oh, it is not. It's perfect. Come on. They're in already." Kristy turned and ran back into the ocean. Mark hated cold water but followed her. He took a deep breath and dove under the next wave.

Fifteen minutes later, Don and Karen walked hand in hand in one direction while Kristy and Mark walked the other way,

"So tell me what's bothering you," said Kristy. She took her hand from Mark's and slid her arm around his waist.

"Hard to imagine anything being wrong in a place like this. It is lovely here."

"Don't wiggle out. What's wrong? Enough, no more. 'Tis not so sweet as it was before. Remember?"

"Did I say that? Perhaps I overdramatized."

Kristy stopped and drew herself up in front of Mark. "Are you going to tell me or not?"

Mark didn't much feel like talking about his personal qualms, but now if he didn't, a chill would descend, and the next five days here in paradise would be much less paradisiacal.

"I'm about to turn twenty-five years old, and I don't have any settled feeling of what I'm doing with my time."

Mollified, Kristy moved alongside Mark and put her arm back around his waist as they walked. "Go on."

"Go on? Well, I can't decide how to best spend my time. What am I supposed to be doing every day to make the day worthwhile?"

"You have the theatre."

"That's Don's department. Theatre is what he takes seriously. It's what fills his every nook and cranny. He knows when he wakes up in the morning what's going to be important to him that day. He studied *Hamlet* for months and played the role with everything he had. Molly

Frederick saw him and took him on. She's working on things for him, not for me. He's unified, single-minded, satisfied with what he's doing."

Kristy leaned her head momentarily on Mark's shoulder. "You write."

"Short stories in a couple of magazines. The two novels spend their time in transit from me to a publisher and then from the publisher back to me. With regrets."

"And if one is published?"

"Well, that might be different. I could happily give my time to writing. Don tells me sometimes he's jealous that I have different interests, a few areas of talent—talent in a loose sense. I used to think he was right, but now I find myself jealous of his being dedicated to one thing, but don't tell him. To let you in on a secret, I did feel focused when I worked on finding out who killed Lawrence. I enjoyed that, if you know what I mean."

"Nice of Mr. Barset to provide you with another murder or two to solve."

Mark shook his head. "Won't happen. We're leaving here in a few days."

They walked in silence for a short distance. An occasional wave provided the accustomed crash as it rolled itself up onto the beach and wet their feet.

Kristy pulled them to another halt. "You don't intend to give up the theatre for writing or detecting, or all three for something else, do you?"

"No, no, but I need something more encompassing than the dabbling I do."

"You're an encompassing lover. An all-encompassing lover." She led him away from the water's edge toward a shoulder-high dune.

"It would be far worse without you, Kristy."

They moved behind the dune. The only things visible were the ocean, the beach, and the dense trees at the sand's end. Kristy put her arms around Mark and kissed him.

"Don mentioned how fetching you and Karen looked in your bathing suits."

"I picked this suit with you in mind, and it's taken you a very long time to comment on it."

"Well, it's hard to speak when one's breath has been taken away. And you moved me into a somber mood—not my fault—but I assure you I did notice. I hereby officially tell you how stupendous you look in your new bathing suit. Turn around and let me drink it in."

Kristy turned coyly, bent slightly, and wiggled. "If you think I look good in my suit..." She slid the bottom of the suit off and tossed it to Mark. "How do I look without it? Help me."

She turned and Mark unhooked the back of her suit. He dropped both pieces onto the sand. Kristy knelt and pulled Mark's suit down.

"Come and join me," she said with a shy smile.

"Join you. You do have a way with words."

The surf continued to move in and out as Kristy and Mark embraced in the warm sand.

Five

Anthony Barset dominated dinner with his talk of Illyria, and kept Ashley and the potential investors—six men, three of whom were Japanese—rapt. Mark swore he saw dollar signs dancing in their eyes. The murders weren't mentioned by Barset or any of the investors. Mark guessed the men had not even been told.

When Barset's sales pitch ended, Mark and the other actors moved away from the table and into the room fronting the beach. The sliding doors and the windows stood wide open as night began to close in. The actors congregated on the left side of the room while the investors clustered around Barset on the right side. He, along with two of the investors, had lit cigars.

Tony Babbitte shook his head. "What are we supposed to do for the next four days? I mean, really. We're not in Kansas anymore. Or New York City, either."

Karen laughed. "At least you'll be eating well for a few days. Enjoy it."

"I admit the dinner was good, but it lacked the panache of a Phebe's chicken rollatini. And, seriously, how can you trust any red wine you can't see through?"

"Stop," Karen ordered, waving off Tony's complaints. "If you can't enjoy anything else, enjoy the weather."

"Weather. What weather?" Tony waved his arm in the direction of the beach. "Every day's the same as every other day here. It won't rain. It won't snow. The temperature won't change. You're going to have to take me home in a pillowcase, I swear. I feel a nervous breakdown looming."

"Here, here, enough of this," Barset bellowed from the other side of the room. "We're having one party here, not two. I promise no more talk of Illyria, beautiful though it is."

The businessmen followed Barset across the room, and the conversational groups integrated to Barset's specifications. Mark and Don found themselves seated in a corner with the great man himself.

"What will you be doing for us Wednesday and Thursday?" he asked before drawing long on his cigar. "Nothing like a good Havana to top off a meal."

Mark and Don declined the offer of a cigar.

"We'll be doing a few scenes from *Hamlet* on Wednesday," Mark explained. "Don made quite a splash in the role at AWB."

"I heard. I heard. Expecting to be swept off to Hollywood soon, so Ashley tells me."

"I wouldn't turn it down. But, yes, I'll be your Hamlet for the evening."

"Wonderful. Wonderful."

"And *Twelfth Night* on Thursday," Mark continued. "That's the play we're opening next week."

Barset leaned over and lowered his voice. "I'll let you in on a little secret. Ashley's mention of your doing *Twelfth Night* gave me the idea of having you down to my little island. Believe it or not, I acted some in college. Didn't keep it up. No money in it—no offense."

"No offense taken," said Mark with a grin. "What were you in?"

"Believe it or not, I played Malvolio." He patted his stomach. "I'm built more like Sir Toby now, but I had a damned fine time with the role, even if I say so myself. After I graduated, though, I decided I'd rather make some money than act. And I did." He smiled. "Anyway, *Twelfth Night* holds a special place for me. When Ashley mentioned it, it struck me to invite her and so you. Now, I have a request to make."

"I'll bet you want to do a scene as Malvolio."

"You are the detective, aren't you, Mark?" Barset remarked, chuckling.

"Which scene? Do you remember it? The lines, I mean," asked Don.

"I do. The very end of the play where Malvolio is brought back on stage to be mocked by the others."

Mark cocked his head, studying his host. "You'll only have one speech plus your exit line."

Barset laughed. "That's about my limit, I assure you, and after your *Hamlet* the night before and whatever scenes you intend to do from *Twelfth Night*, it's best I'm as far to the end with as little to do as possible. I wonder if you'd do me another favor."

"Sure," said Don.

"Ashley, I know, loves to act. Does she have a part in *Twelfth Night*?"

Don shook his head. "No, but she plays a mean Gertrude in *Hamlet*. She'll be doing some of it Wednesday."

"I wonder if she might play Olivia opposite me for that one scene."

Don gave a short laugh. "Sure. It's up to Ashley, of course."

"Let me ask her," said Barset, and he walked away.

"What the hell was that about?" asked Mark.

"You think he's got a crush on Ashley?"

Mark frowned. "No, I don't, but remember, he's trying to pry a wad of cash out of her. Praise is how the theatres back home do it."

"I suppose so,"

Mark looked over the room. With a nod of his head, he indicated Ashley and Barset heading toward the beach through the sliding doors.

"A little moonlight walk on the beach always worked for me," said Don.

"What do you think of the others—the investors?"

Don looked over the six men. "Just your run-of-the-mill pack of millionaires."

"Do those fellows look like they have any great interest in scenes from Shakespeare?"

"No, but Barset's putting on the dog for them. Suppose he invites us to be a permanent Shakespearean troupe here. Scenes from Shakespeare Mondays, Wednesdays, and Fridays for the tourists."

Mark lifted his eyebrows. "What happened to Molly Frederick and Hollywood?"

"I like to have a fallback position."

"You must be Don Lovett and Mark Louis." The speaker was an older man, slim and tanned, who, though dressed in the casual attire one would expect on a tropical island, exuded a sense of elegance and fineness quite missing from everyone else.

"We are," said Don.

"And you are Alexander Overly, I believe," said Mark. "Mr. Barset's partner?"

Overly laughed lightly. "You can remember the hurried introductions over dinner. I'm impressed."

Mark returned the man's smile. "You remembered who we were."

"I confess it is a talent I have, keeping names and faces in order. How did you enjoy your first day in Illyria?"

"A little wilder than we'd imagined," Mark confessed.

"*Ah*, the murder." Overly lowered his voice. "We don't bring it up around our investors-to-be. A word to the wise." He put a quick finger to his lips. "Anthony's brought me up-to-date on everything. I was upstairs working. It seems I'm always upstairs working. You were both with Otavio at the marketplace, I know. It's unimaginable anything so awful could happen here—and repeatedly. I understand from Anthony you're something of a detective?"

"Hardly. I did manage to help Ashley after Lawrence's murder. Did you ever meet him?"

"Once or twice long ago."

"She's had me promise Mr. Barset I'd read over the reports of the three murders, but with so little time and so little information…" Mark punctuated the sentence with a shrug.

"Anthony has the reports on his desk. He meant to deliver them to you before dinner, but the rush of things, you know. I'll be sure you get them tonight. It's in everyone's interest to clear this up."

"I'll read them before I go to bed."

"What will you do then?" asked Overly. "About the investigation, I mean."

"I suppose I should visit the spots where the murders took place."

"You'll need someone to take you around, but Anthony wants to keep the three security people here with his guests."

"What about the young lady who helped serve dinner?" asked Don.

"Ah, yes. You've noticed Nelaneda."

"Nelaneda," Don repeated. "Lovely name."

"A name as lovely as she is. She's depressing to have around, though. The only drawback to the island."

"Drawback? She seems more like a highlight to me."

"To you, yes. If I were your age…what? Twenty-five?"

"Twenty-four."

"…instead of my own age, fifty-six, I might agree. I remember being your age, though, and looking into the eyes of young women like Nelly. You know what I saw? Possibility. The possibility the two of us might end up together. The possibility that a wonderful period of discovery and passion loomed, however brief. I saw it with many women. I can't say every one, of course, but I assure you not a day would go by without that feeling. I could pick and choose where to invest my time.

"Let me tell you what I see when I gaze into the eyes of a young woman now. Nothing. Emptiness. No recognition of me whatsoever. I'm invisible. Not long ago, one young lady told me she felt invaded by the way I looked at her. Invaded, mind you. I consider myself reasonably well-preserved, and I'm very rich. If they know ahead of time I'm rich, there's something in their eyes, but not the look we exchanged when I was in my twenties. Money is irrelevant to that look. But yes, you do right to notice Nelly. I'll suggest she drive you around tomorrow, Mark."

Don waggled finger in the air. "She can drive Mark *and* me around tomorrow. Watson at your service again."

Mark laughed and spoke to Overly. "And language? Any problem?"

"Some natives speak English; most don't. They come from many places. Nelly speaks Spanish and English. I depend on her a lot when I'm here, and I'm here frequently as we try to make Illyria over. She'll be helpful to you."

"Is she...?" Don waited.

"She is available, but Ashley told me you and Miss Christensen are a pair."

"Unofficially. She insists on a relationship that stops short of serious."

It was Alex's turn to waggle a cautionary finger. "Tread cautiously, young man. A woman scorned, no matter what she may have said..."

"Exactly what I told him, Mr. Overly."

"Alex. Call me Alex. Well, I wish you the best of luck, both of you. Anything I can do, of course, just ask. I address that to you only, Mark. Sorry, Don. You're on your own. Now I will go and speak with your Miss Christensen and delude myself into believing she finds me interesting and irresistible."

Don smiled in response. "Be my guest." Overly walked away.

"I like him," said Don.

"He does have a way about him."

"What a pair...an overbearing blob and an entrant in a George Clooney look-alike contest. I wonder if he was ever married. He doesn't sound like he's married now."

"Why don't you ask him?"

"Maybe I will. Oh, look, Barset's back and beckoning us."

"He wants you, Mark. I'm sure he doesn't want Ron."

"This'll be about the reports, I'll bet."

"You go. I'll catch up with you. I'm going to try to strike up a conversation with Nelly."

Mark aped Alex's cautionary scolding. "Be careful. A woman scorned..."

Don rolled his eyes, and the two men parted.

<h1 style="text-align:center">Six</h1>

Mark lay still a moment as the sweet morning breeze, the gentle sound of spent waves, and the call of a seabird began his day. He studied Kristy, breathing softly next to him. She lay on her left side, her face toward him, a thin sheet covering her. Why wouldn't she tell him more of her past? Was she hiding something or merely adding this coyness to her arsenal of allurements? At the moment, it didn't matter. But if they stayed together long enough, it might.

He'd told her he'd be up early and off visiting the scenes of the murders. She told him to go his own way. The beach and ocean held enough adventure for her. He planned to meet Nelly in twenty-five minutes, at eight o'clock—he and Don. He rose without disturbing Kristy and dressed.

Don already sat at the kitchen table, orange juice in hand. "I left Karen sleeping. I told her I'd be off with you this morning."

"With me and Nelly?"

"I left the Nelly part out. I had a chance to talk to Nelly a little last night. Her English is terrific."

"Her first language?"

"I didn't ask. Maybe."

Mark poured himself some juice and sat. "How'd she get here?"

"I didn't get that far; Karen had her eye on me. I guess Barset hired her somehow."

"Is there a point to your paying attention to Nelly?"

"No, I suppose not, but you never know. She is a beauty."

"Here she comes."

Nelly entered the kitchen wearing a loose-fitting white dress with thin shoulder strings, the dress ending some eight inches above her knees. Mark didn't detect much beneath the dress besides Nelly herself. She smiled at Don.

"Nelly, this is my friend Mark."

"Hello, Mark. Where would you like me to drive you today?"

"We want to examine where the three murders happened. Can you find the spots?"

"I can. The people who live on the island are very frightened. Nothing like this has ever happened here. People everywhere on the island look with suspicion at each other. They will be happy to talk to you, but I do not think they will have any helpful information."

Mark rose. "I don't expect to learn anything, Nelly, but I promised our host I'd do this for him. So, the sooner we get started..."

"I am ready," she said brightly.

Don collected the empty juice glasses and put them into the sink. He and Mark followed Nelly outside to one of the jeeps. Don pushed Mark into the back seat, and he settled in to ride shotgun. The jeep was topless, and for a moment Mark watched Nelly's hair whirling backward in the wind. He leaned forward and asked, "Where are we going first?"

Nelly called over her shoulder. "I will show you in order...one, two, three."

Mark settled back and watched the island go by. It was his third trip along the dirt roads of Illyria—once to the marketplace and then back to Barset's home. This one was no more comfortable than the first two. The hard-packed dirt provided enough jolts and jars to fill up a day at an amusement park. The sooner he joined Kristy on Barset's beach to enjoy the water, the sun, and Kristy's backside, the better. Mark had seen only three other cars, and old cars they were, in his other two jaunts around the island, and Nelly drove as if the last thing she expected to encounter was any kind of opposition on the road. She sped around a curve and slid to a halt.

She pointed over the edge of the road as she climbed from the jeep. "This is where the first body was found."

"Down there?" asked Mark.

He and Don followed Nelly off the road and down the incline.

"The body rolled until it became stuck." Nelly indicated the slope ahead. "The murderer cut the throat of the woman, and the blood dripped onto the shack underneath."

The slanting ground ended abruptly. Mark walked to the edge, put his hand against a tree to balance himself, and looked over. Not far below, perhaps twenty feet, was the roof of a shack. A small child played near the shelter. Mark returned to Nelly. "The people who live in the shack found the body?"

"Yes. The blood fell into a basket of fruit sitting near the house. The wife took the fruit inside and saw the blood. The husband investigated."

Mark moved away from the edge of the incline. "So the husband found the body?"

"Yes."

"What happens here when a crime is committed? What did the man do when he found the body?"

"He went and gathered other men. He showed them the body. They carried it to his home. Someone went to Mr. Barset's home. I was there when the man came. Mr. Barset sent Carlos. You have met him?"

Don answered, "Yes, he flew the plane. And what did he do?"

"He asked what happened, and he wrote the report for Mr. Barset."

"Right, the reports," said Don. "Did you read them? Anything helpful in them?"

"Not much more than Nelly's telling us. The dead woman had a husband and a ten-year-old child. Can we talk to the man who found the body?"

"Follow me."

They walked along the road until Nelly found a pathway down to the shack.

The shack looked to Mark like every other shack on the island—some wood, a tin roof, and presto! A home. Nelly gestured for them to wait. "I will see if the husband is here."

She returned a moment later followed by a gaunt man of medium height. He wore loose, baggy trousers and a dull, white, short-sleeved shirt. His sandals were loose over his heels and flopped audibly when he walked.

Nelly translated. "His name is Montez. He says he is glad to meet you."

"Why?"

Nelly spoke a syllable, and the man responded.

"How's your Spanish?" Don asked Mark.

"Don't have any. You?"

"Just New York City leavings. This sounds different from what I know, though."

"He says people who live on the island would not do this to one another. He wants to go with us and look for a stranger. Only a stranger would try to harm people as poor as he and the others."

Mark glanced at the man then at Nelly. "Has he or anyone he knows seen such a stranger?"

Nelly spoke. The man answered. "Everyone is looking, but no, no one has a seen such a stranger."

"Were any of the investors on the island then?"

"Oh, no, no. They only arrived this past Friday."

"Okay. Why don't you tell him if he or anyone else wants to talk to me, I'll be at Barset's house until Friday."

When Nelly spoke this time, alarm, which needed no translation, came into the man's face. He spoke rapidly.

"He wants to know who will protect them when you leave."

"Protect them," said Don. "Who does he think we are?"

"Tell him I will do everything I can."

Mark turned and walked away while Nelly translated. He was seated in the back of the jeep when Don and Nelly caught up with him.

Nelly turned the key in the ignition and paused. "He is worried about his wife and children. This monster, he called him a monster, has killed only women until now. He is afraid children may be killed, also. He thinks you are here because of the murders. He does not understand why you would leave before the killer is discovered."

"Great. Let's go to the next spot."

Mark sat back as Nelly moved the jeep back onto the road.

Mark wondered what the hell he had taken on. He didn't want any part of this. He could give these people sympathy, but they wanted more. They wanted an answer.

When they returned to Barset's house after completing their tour of the three murder sites, Don asked Nelly, "Are you going to the beach today?"

"No, Mr. Barset would not like it. Only when he is not here can I treat the house like my own and use the beach whenever I wish. I must go now. Enjoy your afternoon."

Both men's eyes followed Nelly from the room.

Don sighed. "She is a beauty."

"How the hell can you hope for anything to come of Nelly? You're going to end up with a monumental fight on your hands."

"I know, I know. I'll be careful. Anyway, we've wasted the morning, I presume, at least insofar as finding clues goes."

"You are correct. Let's not waste the afternoon too. Meet you on the beach."

~ * ~

"I'm scorched. I'm roasted. I'm an inhabitant of hell. I hate it here, and I'm going back inside the house forever," Tony Babbitte ranted.

"Jesus, what happened to you?" asked Mark. "You look... illuminated."

He and Don paused in their walk across the sand to join Kristy and Karen in the water when Tony, roasted to a bright pink, staggered up to them. "I fell asleep under that tree. That treacherous freaking tree. That one. And the sun moved."

"I hate to be the one to tell you," said Don. "The sun doesn't move, my friend. The earth moves."

Tony touched his arm with his finger and turned it white for a moment. Everyone watched it ooze back to pink. He lifted his arm and pointed. "The sun was there when I fell asleep, but over there when I woke up. It moved, and I think the damn tree moved, too. It's a conspiracy of nature. And...and I've got this...this stuff all over me."

"It's called sand, Tony."

"I'm leaving. Pick me up on the way to the airport. Good-bye." His neck rigid, Tony walked stiffly across the sand toward the house.

"Ask Nelly to give you something for it," Don called after him.

Tony raised his right hand high, middle finger extended, and plodded ahead to shade and safety.

Don gave a quick laugh. "That may ding him a little."

"I would say so. *Ah,*" said Mark. "They've spotted us."

Kristy and Karen bounded out of the surf and ran toward them. Kristy wore the same suit she'd worn the day before. Karen had on a yellow two-piece suit that displayed her ampleness to marvelous effect. Mark and Don each received a kiss.

Karen pulled Don toward the water. "Come in with me."

Kristy cocked her head at Mark. "How did your morning go?"

Suddenly, Barset's twelve-seat plane ascended from behind the tree line.

"That's Alex," said Kristy. "Anthony's partner."

Mark lifted a brow. "He's flying the plane?"

"He is."

"I didn't know he flew."

"Barset wanted Carlos to fly to St. Thomas for supplies—food and liquor. He wants to be sure to keep the party going."

Mark's gaze followed the plane for a moment. "I see. There's not much else to do on this island."

"Alex volunteered to go. He suggested security should remain at full strength here, what with the guests. And speaking of security, what did you find out this morning?"

He spread his hands in impotence. "These people will break your heart. They lead such simple lives. They have nothing and can't imagine why they're being afflicted with tragedy on top of their poverty. The first victim had a ten-year-old kid. The second cared for an aged parent. The third was young and about to be married. All three were women. All three families are heartbroken— heartbroken and helpless. They can't imagine who would do something like this or why, and neither can I."

"Are there any connections between the three families, the three people?"

"None apparent to me." He sighed. "Oh God, if I felt gloomy before, I'm full-scale depressed now."

Kristy pursed her lips. "You'd like to do something about this, wouldn't you?"

"I would. Damn, I feel so...earnest. But I suppose there is an upside. These poor people face problems that make ours—yours, mine—look like nothing. They literally have to worry about where their next meal is coming from."

"We still have a few days. Maybe you'll come up with something. You aren't going to let it get you down, are you? I mean further down."

He looked into her face. She smiled and the full wonder of her washed over him. His eyes roved down her body and back up again.

"I usually smack men who leer at me like that," she said. "But in your case, I'll make an exception."

"I realize how much worse it would be without you. I do." He stepped closer and embraced her. "I'm no doubt feeling some momentary burst of insecurity left over from adolescence, but I'll get over it. Kiss me."

She obeyed.

He stepped back and took a breath. "Where are the investors?"

"Barset is showing them architectural plans, I think. He's got this whole island mapped out, designed, and booked through next Christmas, I'll bet."

Mark heard his name and turned.

"Ashley," said Kristy.

"What in the world has her so excited?"

Ashley summoned him with repeated gestures.

"You'd better go."

Mark jogged across the soft sand until he heard Ashley say, "Mark, they've caught the killer. He murdered someone a little while ago, but the people saw him and caught him."

"Now? Just now?"

"Yes. Someone came to the house and told Adiba. Carlos and the other security people are getting ready to leave, and I thought you'd want to go along. They're waiting for you."

"Yes, I do want to go. Will you tell Kristy where I went?"

"Of course. They're waiting for you in front of the house."

He ran up the stairs two at a time and threw on a shirt. He slid into an old pair of moccasins he'd packed and in three minutes time was again speeding along the dirt roads of Illyria.

The murder had occurred near the marketplace—too near. The jeep Mark rode in slowed to navigate the crowds of shoppers then sped up. Thirty seconds later, his vehicle and the lead jeep spun to a stop.

"Is this where it happened?" he asked Carlos.

Carlos slid from behind the steering wheel. "Yes. The body is still here." He pointed to a knot of natives standing in the distance. The ground on both sides of the road was open here for some distance before the tropical trees dominated again. The crowd clustered well in front of the tree line.

Mark had to run to keep up, and the natives stepped away when Carlos and Barset's other two men bore down on them. An old white sheet covered the body.

Carlos talked to the natives, and Mark moved closer to the corpse. He took a breath, squatted, and lifted the corner of the sheet.

Under it lay an old man whose neck was gashed, the ground beneath him stained with blood. Mark replaced the sheet and walked away for a few moments to collect himself.

When he turned back to the crowd of people, Carlos had a native by the arm, escorting him away. The native's hands were tied behind him with a thick rope. Barset's other two security men, Otavio and Haniel, walked alongside. The native who had come to the Barset house to report the murder talked to the gathering. Carlos stopped and barked something at him in Spanish, and he grew quiet.

Mark drew alongside Carlos as he escorted the captive toward the jeep. "What's going on? What did you say to that man?"

"They have an idea of immediate justice," Carlos explained, moving even faster. "I discouraged him. We cannot allow such a thing. There are many more of them than there are of us, however, and more are gathering."

Mark stopped when they reached the jeep. Carlos pushed the captive into the back seat and climbed in next to him. Haniel leaped into the driver's seat and started the engine. A moment later he maneuvered the jeep through the marketplace and continued back to Barset's house.

Otavio, the remaining guard, motioned for Mark to climb into the second jeep.

Mark paused. "Can we talk to these people for a minute?"

"They are in an ugly mood," Otavio said in his island-accented English.

"We'll be fine now the murderer's been taken away. They can't very well get to him now. Let's walk back."

Otavio looked unsure but followed Mark down the road. When they reached the crowd, Mark said, "Ask them what happened."

Otavio spoke to the mostly male crowd, first in English then in Spanish. Two men stepped forward. "These are the men who make the capture."

Mark saw fear lingering in their eyes. "Can we take them back to Barset's house for a while? Will they come?"

"I will ask." Otavio addressed the men again in Spanish. The men spoke together. Finally, with a nod, they agreed.

Mark motioned to the jeep. The men walked forward and took the two rear seats.

"*Gracias,*" Mark said, climbing in front. "Let's go, Otavio, before anything happens to change their minds."

Otavio started the engine and headed back to Barset's.

When Mark reached the house, he found only his fellow actors in the living room.

"Anti-climactic entrance," Don remarked. "What kept you? They already locked the bad guy up." He pointed in the direction of a shed visible outside.

"Who have you brought back?" asked Marty.

"Whoever they are, you'll have to excuse me," said Tony, "but Dr. Gideon Fell is about to uncover a fictitious murderer. Much more interesting and understandable, no offense. I'll retire to my room with my book. Bringing your book, Marty?"

"No, I think I'll stay and listen."

Tony got up, moaned slightly, and walked stiff-legged from the room.

"So who are they?" Marty asked again.

"These two gentlemen caught the murderer," Mark explained. "I wanted to talk to them, and, thankfully, they accepted my invitation to come back with us."

"I am sorry, sir," Otavio said. "I had better go to Carlos and help with the guarding."

Mark nodded toward the two natives. "I'll need someone to translate for me."

"Maybe we can have Nelly do it," suggested Don.

"I will send her here." Otavio turned and left.

Mark returned to the two natives and motioned for them to sit down. "I wonder if we can get them something to eat."

"I'll go and find Adiba," said Kristy. "He'll bring something."

"Good. Thanks."

"So what happened?" asked Don.

"I don't know yet. These fellows must have seen something. They managed to capture the killer before he got away."

Don studied the two natives. "They're not very inspiring. Where's the body?"

"Back near the marketplace. The natives'll take care of it, I suppose."

Nelly entered the room. "Did you want me to help you?" She looked at Don when she spoke.

Karen put her hand on Don's shoulder. "Why don't we sit down and let Mark go about his business?"

Don held his ground for a moment, but in the end, he followed Karen to a sofa on the other side of the living room.

"Nelly, will you translate for me?"

"Of course."

"Ask them their names."

The two natives were older men, thin and unhealthy looking. They answered Nelly's question. "This is Cohiba, and this is Fernand."

"Ask them to tell me what happened today."

She spoke a sentence or two, which elicited an outpouring of explanation from the two men, often simultaneously. Mark saw it would take her a while to get the whole story for him, so he moved his chair into a more comfortable position from which to hold this conversation and waited.

"How long is this thing going to take?" asked Don. "We haven't had lunch yet."

"Why don't you go help Kristy find Adiba?" suggested Karen. "Ask him to fix everyone something."

"Uh, sure." Don rose and left the room, tossing Mark a knowing glance when he passed behind Karen.

Mark rose from his chair and walked to the open window. A pleasant breeze greeted him, along with the smell of the ocean. He turned back to face the room. Nelly and the two natives continued to converse. He walked over to join Karen on the sofa, but before he sat down, Nelly and the two men stopped talking and looked his way.

"Do you have their story?"

"Yes."

"Let's wait for Don and Kristy. Anyone want a drink?"

"If there's a beer," said Karen.

"Beer sounds good," Marty agreed.

"I will get some for everyone." Nelly walked behind the wet bar in the corner. The two native men nodded when Nelly addressed them, and she began to distribute beers from a small refrigerator.

Kristy and Don returned.

"Adiba is fixing us something," Don announced. "We ready?"

Everyone found places, and Nelly got two additional beers for Don and Kristy.

"Here is their story," Nelly said, sitting down. The hiss of spent waves provided the only background to her voice. "Cohiba and Fernand are brothers. They sell cabbages in the market. Cohiba had left the stall to go home to get their lunch. He began walking up the pathway toward his home. He had gone no more than..."

She turned to Cohiba and spoke. He answered. "...thirty seconds down the road when he heard someone running through the brush. The running went past him toward the market. He walked another few seconds, he says. There, on the ground, he saw an old man and ran to him. The old man's eyes were open, and he tried to speak, but he died quickly. Cohiba remembered the running feet and ran back toward the market. When he neared the open space of the market, he saw a man standing, hiding...what is the word...?"

"Lurking?" Don suggested.

Nelly shrugged. "Hiding behind a tree. Their eyes met, he said, and the man gave him a look of craziness or anger. The man leaped over the bushes toward him, and Cohiba saw he had a large knife. Cohiba ran toward the marketplace calling for his brother. He reached the end of the trees and bushes where it opens into the marketplace. Not only his brother heard him, but many merchants and other people heard him, too. They started his way. Cohiba ran ahead, and the man with the knife followed him to the marketplace. Those coming toward Cohiba saw the man and what he carried. They called to the others following behind. The man with the knife turned and ran away. Cohiba and his rescuers—more than twenty men—chased after the man with the knife, but when they caught him, he didn't have the knife. They found it in the grass where he had dropped it or thrown it. They held him, and Fernand sent someone to inform Mr. Barset. You know the rest."

When she stopped talking, Mark looked at the two men, who stood quietly drinking their beer. "Is there anything else they can add?"

"Do you have a question you would like me to ask them?"

"Did they recognize this man, the one they caught?"

Nelly put the question. "No, they say the man is a stranger."

"I wonder if Mr. Barset will let me question the prisoner."

"I will go to the beach and ask him if you want."

"Would you, Nelly? Thanks."

Adiba appeared in the room and announced lunch.

"Do we ask these two gentlemen to join us?" asked Mark.

"No, no," said Nelly. "They will eat in the kitchen. Adiba will bring your food here."

"How do we get them home?"

"I will go and tell Mr. Barset what you want to do, and after they eat, I will drive them back to the marketplace." Nelly spoke to the two men a moment, and they left the room.

Adiba brought in a large tray with five plates. Lunch was a small piece of fish, some green beans, and rice. They sat around the table and ate.

"This murder seems to be different from the others, doesn't it?" asked Mark.

Don lowered his fork. "How? The guy slipped up. This time someone happened along. It could have happened any of the other three times."

"He was too close to the marketplace," said Kristy. "But I'm surprised no one knows him. When was the first murder? A while ago, right? He must have been here at least since then."

"Three weeks." Mark tapped the table with his index finger. "He'd have to have been on the island for at least three weeks. There's no way he could commit a murder and leave the island, return and commit another murder."

"He seems crazy enough to be a killer," Marty interjected.

"When I talk to him, we'll see how crazy he is."

Nelly returned and said, "I have spoken with Mr. Barset. He has told Carlos to expect you."

Everyone ate quickly, and when they finished, they rose from the table, left the house, and followed Nelly to the shed.

"You want to speak to this man?" asked Carlos, rising from a canvas chair.

"I do," answered Mark. "I brought reinforcements with me."

"Do not worry. We will be safe."

Haniel and Otavio stood behind Mark as he unlocked the shed door. The bright sunlight reached into the shed far enough to illuminate the captured man's drawn-up knees as he sat against the back wall. He covered his face with his hands at the introduction of the light but stayed seated. Carlos spoke to him in Spanish. The man rose and stepped toward the open door. The man, sweating profusely, stopped in the doorway and crossed his arms.

Carlos turned to Mark. "What would you like me to ask him?"

"Ask him whether he committed this murder."

Carlos put the question, and the man answered. "He says he did. God instructed him to."

"God instructed him to? I see. Ask him whether he committed the other three murders."

Carlos put the question to the man. "He says God will not permit His secrets to be known to someone like you."

"Ask when God began speaking to him."

Carlos translated. "He says he is special and a chosen one of God. God speaks to such as him."

"Let's try it this way. Ask how long he's been on Illyria?"

"Long enough to feel the evil here, he says. He says he will stay here until the evil is removed from the island."

"We're not going to get a sensible answer from this guy," said Don.

"Is there anything else you would like me to ask him?"

"Where did he live before he came to this island?"

"He says in a big country far away."

Mark shook his head. "This is no use."

Carlos ordered the man back inside and locked the door.

"What do we do now?" asked Kristy.

"Thanks, Carlos."

Mark and the others started back toward the house. "There's nothing I can think of. Alex will take this guy off to St. Thomas tomorrow, and that will be the end of it, I guess."

"I didn't mean what to do about him. I meant, isn't it about time to get back to the beach?"

"The beach gets my vote," said Karen.

"I hear my exit cue," said Marty. "I'll see you at dinner. And after dinner maybe we can rehearse a little. We're on the next two nights, you know. I'd like to rehearse once at least."

Mark cracked a smile. "That should please Tony. Remind him of home a little. Okay, the rest of you—into costumes. Bathing suits, that is. The rest of the afternoon is ours."

~ * ~

The next morning after breakfast, the acting company, Ashley excepted, sat on the veranda behind Barset's house.

"It's going to be hotter than hell today." Tony shifted his position and grimaced. "This shade is miraculous for as long as it lasts."

"And wasn't last night grand?" said Marty. "We rehearsed. We acted again. I find I missed it. To me, this life of unmitigated ease leaves a lot to be desired."

Don nodded. "I admit the rehearsing did feel good."

"We'll do the four scenes from *Hamlet* tonight and four from *Twelfth Night* tomorrow," said Marty. "Then back to New York and civilization and an opening night."

"Here, here," mumbled Tony.

"Did Barset and Ashley rehearse their scene last night?" Don rubbed sweat from the side of his neck. "They didn't rehearse with us. There are other people in their scene. We should run through that once, too."

"They partied with the investors all night," said Kristy.

"What's the money doing today?" asked Karen.

Mark moved his chair out of the creeping sunlight. "Barset is taking them to some scenic lagoon. Ashley's going with them. I'll suggest she and Barset go through the scene once before tomorrow night, if not with the whole cast, at least with each other. Otherwise it might come off as ludicrous."

Karen gave a long stretch. "So we have nothing to do today. Wonderful."

"Don't suggest the beach, please," Tony whined. "This sand stuff doesn't come off once it gets on you. It's disgusting. I won't even mention where I found some of it. Why don't we rehearse some more? Like all day."

Mark smiled as everyone greeted Tony's suggestion with a ponderous silence, and soon another day on the beach commenced—without Marty and Tony, who retired to the house.

~ * ~

The four scenes from *Hamlet* played to general acclaim.

Barset led the applause and followed up with a toast.

"To our talented friends from New York. Poor Alex had to remain an extra day on St. Thomas and will only hear reports of their wonderful performance. But he stayed for a good reason. He had to do quite a bit of work there because four of our investors have decided to join me in making this island into a tropical paradise, a money-making tropical paradise."

Mark could tell from the intensity of the smiles which four investors had bought in and which two hadn't.

"Alex will be back early tomorrow morning. He knows he'll have to make another flight to finally remove a murderer from the island, so we have every reason to celebrate. Please, drink up."

"Millions of dollars, just like that," Mark said to Ashley as he enjoyed his first drink of the evening. "It's hard to comprehend." He, along with the other actors, had changed back into their tropical island clothes from the basic stage costumes they'd brought along with them. Nelly served drinks while everyone spread out in the large, comfortable living room overlooking the beach.

"Yes, I'm beginning to wonder whether I shouldn't perhaps invest something more than I'd planned," said Ashley. "I will tell you, Mark, I've come to consider myself a rich woman, but next to these people, I'm quite put in my place."

Mark cleared his throat. "I may be out of line, but how much were you going to invest in Illyria?"

"I felt comfortable risking only a few million. But now, I'm not so sure. I'll have to mull it over." She sipped her white wine and looked over the room. "Why don't you join Kristy? She seems to be having too good a time with that young rich investor."

Mark laughed and took a few steps but turned back. "Ashley, if you and Mr. Barset are going to do a scene tomorrow night, you both should go through it once or twice."

"Yes, Anthony mentioned it to me. He suggested we rehearse it tomorrow some time. Here's Anthony now. Anthony, Mark insists we go through our scene for tomorrow night."

"And indeed we shall, tomorrow morning. We must keep up the high quality of Illyrian theatrical performances. Great work tonight, Mark."

"I'm glad you enjoyed it, Mr. Barset. We're happy to repay your hospitality in any way we can."

Barset brought the talk back to where he seemed to prefer it. "We'll soon have the capital we need and get started. If we can persuade O'Brian and Cohen, and you, too, Ashley, to come aboard, we'll be in superior shape. I knew from the start that our Japanese friends would lead the way." He tapped his temple with an index finger. "Smart."

"Did they enjoy our scenes from Shakespeare?" asked Mark.

"They haven't stopped talking about it. They've studied English literature to some degree. Two have even studied Shakespeare, but they said they've never had an experience like the one you provided tonight."

"High praise. You'll have to bring them to the Bouwerie Lane Theatre if they get to New York."

"You can count on it."

"I'll leave you two alone," said Mark.

"Be assured I will get Ashley into rehearsal first thing tomorrow. I promise you that."

Seven

The next day, Mark and the other actors directed various sympathetic comments toward Alex Overly, about to make his second flight to the isle of St. Thomas, this time with a murderer in tow.

Alex waved off their concern. "I'll be back in plenty of time to join you on the beach. And you don't know how sorry I am to have missed last night's performance. I promise I won't miss tonight's. The authorities are meeting me at the airport. Transferring this fellow shouldn't take too long. Besides, I wouldn't miss Anthony's acting debut for the world."

Barset appeared at the doorway to the kitchen where Alex, Don, and Mark were having juice, and he beckoned to Alex.

"If I don't see you before I leave," Alex said to Don and Mark, "save me a nice, warm spot on the sand."

"Will do," Don assured him. "So let's not waste a moment." He directed this comment to Mark as Alex left the room. "Tomorrow we're out of here and back to freezing New York, and we won't get to ogle a bathing suit-clad beach bunny for months."

"Let's go wake up the ladies."

Twenty minutes later, as Barset's plane roared overhead, Nelly and Adiba brought out the bacon, eggs, and buttered toast that constituted the morning's feast. Two people had not yet come down from their bedrooms—an unconvinced investor, Kevin O'Brian, and Ashley. Plus, Barset hadn't returned after calling Alex away earlier.

Don commented to Mark on Ashley and Barset's absence. "You don't think they've paired off, do you? They did disappear down the beach together last night."

"Get serious. After Lawrence, Ashley's hardly ready for another relationship."

"Who said anything about a relationship?"

"A passionate one-night stand? Here? Now? No, I don't think so."

Don nodded his head in the direction of the doorway. Barset and O'Brian entered the room, looking pleased with one another.

Barset announced, "Good morning. Good morning. We have another commitment for our Illyria project. Kevin has decided to join our great venture. Things are looking better and better day by day."

A brief burst of laughter and applause ensued, and breakfast resumed.

"Ashley must have worn herself out last night," said Karen.

"Worn out? What do you mean?" asked Mark.

"She went out again after her walk on the beach with Mr. Barset. Remember, I stayed downstairs after you folks went to bed? She said she didn't want to waste a minute of such a glorious night."

"Anybody see her come in or hear her this morning?" asked Mark.

No one had.

"Kristy, why don't you go up and knock on her door. Tell her she's missing breakfast."

Kristy lowered her fork. "You don't think anything happened, do you?"

Don gulped the last of his orange juice. "Mark, the killer is ten thousand feet in the air."

"So where is she?"

Karen stood. "I'll go with you, Kristy."

Don looked after the departing women before turning to Mark. "What do you think?"

"It's nothing, I'm sure. We'll know in a minute."

"We'll know what? The crazy guy's halfway to St. Thomas by now and was locked in the shed last night. Are you not telling Watson everything?"

Mark took a mouthful of scrambled eggs and didn't answer.

"So be inscrutable. You're more Charlie Chan than Sherlock Holmes. Oh, they're back."

Mark couldn't misinterpret the worried looks on the faces of the two women as they took their seats at the table.

Through the morning chatter of the other diners, Kristy reported, "She doesn't answer her door. We knocked and knocked."

"Didn't you go in?" asked Don.

"We tried. It's locked," Karen answered.

"What do you think, Mark?" Kristy asked.

"We'll have to get inside the room. I'll tell Barset." He rose.

"Let's not stay behind," said Don, and he and the two women followed Mark from the room.

When they found Barset, he looked askance at Mark's asking him where they could find Ashley, but an incipient smile disappeared as Mark continued to explain.

"We have to look inside her room," Mark insisted. "I'm telling you, something's not right about this supposed lunatic doing the killings; I wasn't sure whether I should mention it or not. But Ashley should either be down here eating or still in bed."

"She should be. She should be. I agree," said Barset. "But you must be wrong about our incarcerated friend. Let's go see about Ashley. I'm sure she won't mind if we wake her—or peek into her room, at any rate." He waved his hand toward Nelly. "Come with us, Nelly, and bring your keys." The group of six went upstairs to Ashley's room.

"Open the door," Barset commanded.

Nelly went through her ring of keys until she found the one she wanted. She inserted the key, pushed the door open, and stepped back.

Everyone crowded through the doorway and stared at the rumpled bedclothes.

A voice came from behind them. "I hope the resort you're planning on provides a bit more privacy than this."

"Ashley!" cried Barset.

She faced them with her hands on her hips. "Yes, Ashley. Missing breakfast must be a high crime on Illyria to cause this."

After a momentary pause, Barset said, "We wondered what detained you."

"Six of you? I'm honored. Can we go downstairs now? I got up early and decided to walk the beach again now that we're safe. It is such a beautiful island." She entwined her arm through Barset's as she led him and the others from her room.

"What school did you learn detecting in?" Don whispered to Mark as they followed in the wake of the older couple. "Elementary?"

Mark ignored him.

The dining room had emptied, and Adiba was busy cleaning up.

"I'll have juice and some fruit," Ashley said, waving off Adiba's offer of a fuller breakfast. "We have a few chores to do ourselves today, Anthony."

"I know what one of them is," he said with a wink. "A rehearsal for tonight's performance."

"Yes, it should be a lot of fun. But I'll take your suggestion first. I want to see the marketplace. I haven't been there yet. The more I see Illyria, the more beautiful it looks and the more I like it. I do love walking the beach."

"I'm happy to hear it."

"We'll talk a little business also."

Barset beamed. "Business is always welcome."

"It must be our time for the beach," said Kristy.

"The investor types have beaten us there," said Karen. "The first day they did that."

"I'm game," Mark agreed.

"Go, go, go," Barset urged. "It's your last day. Tonight is our final party. Enjoy. Come with me, Ashley, darling. Let's make your last day here an enjoyable one. After our rehearsal, I'll take you to the marketplace. I'm at your service."

~ * ~

Hours later at two o'clock, the drone of an engine overhead made Mark look skyward. Barset's airplane was returning. "So Alex won't miss a day on the beach," he said.

Barset cleared his throat. "Alex didn't go. Carlos is flying the plane. Otavio went with him."

Mark turned to Barset. "Didn't go? I thought he took the murderer back to St. Thomas."

"I had to keep him on the island today. There's so much work—what with the new investors. He's up in his room going over papers. Besides, he'd just made the trip so he didn't mind letting the others handle the man we caught."

From the corner of his eye, Mark saw Tony slogging his way toward them through the sand and wondered what would bring him onto the beach.

"What's up?" Mark called to him.

"Haniel's back. He says he couldn't find Ashley. She wasn't where they planned to meet. He waited fifteen minutes then went to look for her."

"And he didn't find her?" Mark asked in surprise.

"No," Tony said. "He said she was nowhere to be found."

Kristy shrugged. "She must have taken a longer walk than she planned."

"Haniel says no. She promised to meet him in the marketplace at one-thirty."

Barset joined the conversation. "What's wrong?"

"It's Ashley," Mark explained. "She didn't show up to meet Haniel."

Barset checked his watch and looked at Tony. "She should have met him half an hour ago. He couldn't find her at all?"

"That's what he says. When she didn't show up, he went looking for her."

"Haniel should have stayed and waited. She's probably there now, wondering why I forgot to send someone. Thank God that maniac is off the island. I'd better go and get her."

"Could she be lost?" asked Kristy.

"Not for long. This is a small island, but I suppose she might get confused and wander around for a while. Haniel and I will take both jeeps. We'll find her."

"I'd like to come," said Mark.

"By all means. The rest of you can go about your business. Mark and I will find her."

"Okay. Hurry back," said Kristy.

Mark followed Barset across the sand and around to the front of the house. Barset took the driver's seat and Mark climbed in next to him. Haniel followed in a second jeep.

When they reached the marketplace, Barset stopped and pointed. "She said she preferred to wander around by herself. I advised her to walk along that road. Let's drive down it and look for her." The two jeeps moved ahead slowly.

After a fruitless forty minutes, Mark said, "Mr. Barset, I'd like to take a jeep and look elsewhere."

"She planned to walk down here," Barset said distractedly. "Yes, of course. Go with Haniel. I'll keep looking along here."

Mark took his place next to Haniel and directed him back to the marketplace. "Stop here a minute," he ordered. "Can you ask around at the stalls whether they noticed an older woman with long white hair take any of these other paths?"

Mark remained behind while Haniel went stall to stall. After Haniel had a prolonged talk with one proprietor, he hustled back to the car. "The fruit seller say an older woman with long white hair go down the road behind his stall."

"Where does it lead?"

"To the ocean. All roads lead to the ocean."

"Let's drive along it."

The road ended after half-a-mile. Beyond the end of the road, a rocky incline began. Mark left the jeep.

The sea crashed dramatically against huge boulders at the base of the incline. Off to the right of the road, the same incline led to a rocky beach.

Mark peered over the edge into the sea. He walked along the summit toward the right and stopped. Ashley's body sprawled atop a craggy rock far below him.

~ * ~

Kristy handed Mark a heavy vodka and tonic. "How did it happen?" They sat with Don and Karen on the veranda in the rear of Barset's house. Mark took a breath and began. "Barset says she didn't go in the direction he suggested to her. She went the opposite way. She must have wandered too close to the edge. The rocks are loose along the precipice of the hill there. She must have lost her balance, her traction, on the loose gravel and tumbled over."

"Poor old lady," Karen said softly. "Horrible. What's happens now?"

"Barset sent a boat to retrieve the body. I suppose it'll be flown back to New York."

"In the plane with us?" Karen asked.

"I don't think so," said Don. "I hope not. Will it?"

"We'll all find out together," said Mark.

"Just think," said Kristy. "If the murderer hadn't been caught, Ashley would never have left the house to take those walks. Imagine! Catching the murderer was more dangerous to Ashley than having him free."

Alex Overly stepped onto the veranda from the house. "I heard voices here. It's not a time to be alone."

"Aren't the investors inside?" asked Mark.

"I prefer to be with people who knew Ashley. Anthony knew her better than I, but I did know her."

"Are they flying the body back on the same plane we're taking over?" asked Karen.

"No, no. I'll be flying the body over tomorrow morning. I'll make arrangements for its transport back to the States. Afterward, I'll come back here and pick you up. Your plane from St. Thomas isn't until three, right? I see the boat returning. I'll go out to help." He nodded a farewell and left.

"It'll be a long time until tomorrow," said Kristy.

"I'm getting a headache from this," Karen complained. "I'm going in to lie down."

"Maybe I'll follow Alex," said Don. "One of us should be there. Mark?"

"I'll catch up with you in a while."

When Mark and Kristy were alone, he asked, "Will you come with me for the rest of the afternoon?"

"Where to?"

"Back to where Ashley fell. I want to look around."

"If you want me to. What are you looking for?"

"Don't know."

"You thought the final murder was different from the other murders, didn't you?"

"I did."

Kristy touched Mark's elbow. "So what aren't you telling me? Since you came back from visiting the murder scenes with Don and Nelly, you've been preoccupied."

"These murders, these people have been on my mind."

"What aren't you telling me, Mark darling?" her voice lifting higher.

Mark took Kristy's hand from his elbow and kissed her palm. "Kristy darling, the man's face when we told him we might be leaving before dealing with these murders...I can't get it out of my mind. It's as if I came here looking for some kind of serious, full-time obligation, and now one is thrust upon me, and I'm leaving tomorrow."

"Some are born obligated, some achieve obligations, and some have obligations thrust upon 'em."

"*Hmmm.* With a little editing, Shakespeare has a quote for everything, doesn't he?"

"And what is your obligation now?"

"First, to be certain Ashley's throat wasn't cut, and, secondly, to satisfy myself Ashley's death was the accident it appears."

"And if it's not?"

"And if it's not, to find out who killed her and why."

Eight

The usual opening night butterflies danced within Mark. No one from the troupe had been in favor of postponing *Twelfth Night*, and at Ashley's service earlier that day, Mark had grown tired of hearing people say, "Ashley would have wanted it that way."

By evening's end, he knew that, thanks to a full house, both players and audience managed the willing suspension of grief, and the spirit of the play came through. Although they cancelled their opening night party, the actors did gather at Phebe's.

"Did I hear our Illyrian investors are attending tomorrow's show?" Don asked as he, Mark, Kristy, and Karen settled around a table for four.

"They'll be here," Mark confirmed. "Marty got a call today from Barset. Barset said Gehring wanted to talk to us." Gehring was Ashley's lawyer. She'd made him available at her own expense to the members of the company when the police questioned them back in November after the murder of Lawrence Mickelman.

"Who is us?" asked Kristy.

"The company."

"I wonder why," said Don.

"Probably about the will. Ashley's will is going to be read on Saturday afternoon, you know."

"Be nice if she left her money to the theatre," said Don. "If she didn't leave us something, we're cooked."

"True enough," Mark agreed. "But it's not the will that's bothering me."

Kristy managed a weak smile. "I didn't know anything had been bothering you. I mean more than usual."

Mark looked at each of his friends in turn. "I want to tell you about what happened on Illyria. Kristy and I went back to where Ashley fell."

"We didn't find anything," said Kristy. "You didn't mention you saw anything out of the ordinary."

"It didn't hit me right away. It wasn't what we found. It's what we didn't find. What did Ashley take with her the morning she left with Barset? Any of you remember?"

Mark gave his audience time to replay the morning in their minds. Finally, Don said, "Didn't she have a camera with her?"

"Yes," said Kristy. "She did. A pretty fancy one, as I recall."

"So where is the camera?" asked Mark.

"In the ocean?" Don suggested. "Must be. Or else smashed to smithereens on the rocks."

"Essentially right on both counts. I went back the next morning alone before we left the island to try and find it, and I did find a major chunk of it on the beach, either tossed there by the water, or it fell and ended up there. Anyway, the brains of it were retrievable." Mark reached into the small shopping bag he'd brought with him from the theatre. He tossed an envelope of photographs onto the table.

"You got pictures out of it?" Don took the envelope and dealt the photos out on the table.

"They're spoiled," said Karen.

Mark answered, "The damage from the fall and the ocean water didn't do the camera any good, that's for sure, but the guy at the drug store did his best. Look at them closely, though. Some are better than others."

Mark waited while a new round of intense study began. Kristy tapped a photo. "Isn't this Ashley?"

"Let me see," said Karen. She twisted the picture back and forth. "It looks like it might be her."

Don agreed. "It's Ashley. So?"

"Let me see," said Mark. "This is the final picture taken. Can you make out the background? Examine it carefully." He watched the foggy, imperfect image pass from hand to hand.

"I know what it is," said Kristy.

Don looked at her. "I do, too."

"Well, I must be dense," said Karen. "What is it? Where is it?"

Kristy said, "It appears to be Ashley's standing on the edge of the incline where she fell."

"That's what I think," said Mark.

"You mean to say she fell trying to position herself for a photo?"

"That's not the point, Karen," said Mark.

"What is the point?"

"The point is—who took the picture?" Mark scanned the faces of his friends as a moment of silent surprise washed over the table.

"Someone was with her," said Don.

"Clearly," said Mark.

"A native?" Kristy guessed.

"You and I asked around the day we went back to the scene," said Mark.

"How'd you manage to talk to them?" asked Don.

"We spoke with the ones who knew English, and they spoke to the ones who didn't," Kristy explained. "No one saw her anywhere near the spot where she fell."

"But someone took this picture," said Mark. "Someone who hasn't come forward."

"Who could it have been?" asked Karen. "Maybe someone happened by, and she asked for help. The person might not even know what happened afterward."

Mark looked at Karen. "In what language did she ask for help?"

"Lots of the people speak English," Karen argued. "You said you found some in the marketplace. Or maybe sign language would have been enough. All the person needed to do was push a button."

Mark leaned back. "Well, I'd sure like to find out who pushed that button."

"Couldn't she set the camera to snap a picture automatically?" asked Karen.

"No. There was nothing around to set the camera on. Not at the height necessary to get this shot."

"Fingerprints on the camera!" Don exclaimed as if he'd achieved a major insight.

"I thought of that too late—after I saw the photos and knew there had to be a second person. I'd already handled the camera to a fare-thee-well. So, probably, had the fellow who developed the photos."

"Where's the camera now?" asked Don.

"I still have what's left of it."

Kristy moved the topic away from Mark's mishandling of the camera. "Anything else?"

"This one might be stretching it a bit. You tell me, Kristy. You were there. Describe the ground near the edge where Ashley slipped and fell."

"Rocks, pebbles, dirt, a few boulders, a sprinkling of wild flowers and weeds part of the way down. Then a sheer drop."

"If someone began slipping, what would be their natural reaction?"

Don answered. "Try to find something to hold onto."

"And if you were scrambling to find a handhold, and you were sliding away, dirt would get on your hands, under your fingernails, on the front, sides, of your clothes." Mark raised his eyebrows looking for concurrence.

"Sounds right," Don murmured.

"Ashley's hands, fingernails, and dress were dirt free."

"How do you know?" asked Don.

"I went into the living room after everyone went to bed. I inspected the body and the clothes more closely."

Kristy gasped. "Oh, Mark."

"It would indicate she didn't slide and fall but rather left the edge cleanly and soared out into space. Anyway, that's how it looks to me."

A quiet moment went by as Mark awaited a reaction.

Kristy finally spoke. "So you're saying someone took her picture near the edge of the hill, walked over and handed her back the camera, then pushed her out into space?"

"It fits the facts we've laid out, doesn't it?"

"She still could have slipped, though," said Karen. "It's still possible, isn't it?"

"I don't see how, without the slightest trace of dirt on her hands or her clothing. She flew from the edge and fell onto the boulder where we found her."

"What a horrible thought," Kristy muttered. "Anything else?"

"Only something I said on the island. The final murder of a native differed from the first three."

"Differed how?" asked Kristy.

"The first three victims were women; the fourth, an old man. The first three murders happened far enough away from the marketplace or so early in the day there was little possibility of someone happening along. The last one happened close to the marketplace around lunchtime when people were bound to be around. Also, what about the poor lunatic who did the final killing? How could he run around acting like he acted for three weeks, a month, and not be noticed? He'd have to be incredibly lucky to commit murder after murder as carelessly as the final one and not be caught. No, I see something quite different going on in the first three killings. I wish I'd had more time to poke around on the island."

"I'm ready to fly back," Kristy said with a smile.

"Count me in," said Karen.

"So what do you do now?" asked Don.

"We can't go back to the island without Barset's approval and patronage," said Mark. "I wish we could."

"Hold it. Hold it. Watson to the rescue. Why don't you call Nelly? She's always there. Ask her to ask around. She'd do it for us, I bet." Don's face clouded. "Unless you think it'd be dangerous."

"I wouldn't even know how to contact her."

"Do you have her number?" Karen asked, looking at Don.

"Me? No, but we could ask Barset for it."

Mark spread his hands. "It's a possibility. There's nothing else to do until we talk to Barset. Might as well order another round and get a bit of food to nibble on. There must be happier things to discuss."

"Good idea," said Karen.

Don smiled at her and beckoned the waiter.

Nine

Don and Mark were the members of the AWB Theatre Company asked to attend the reading of the will. As they walked down the red-carpeted hallway of Gehring, Levinson, and Marchi on Park Avenue, Mark heard Anthony Barset's booming laughter.

"He sounds happy enough," said Mark. "Maybe Ashley left her money to him." He opened the door to the lawyers' office.

"Ah, you're here," Barset said, offering a big smile as they entered a waiting area. "Sorry I had to run last night, but I'm showing my new partners around, and we had dinner plans." Barset and two of his Japanese partners, Brian Takeda and Kevin Yoshi, had attended AWB's second performance of *Twelfth Night*. They'd stopped backstage to offer their compliments before rushing off.

"Will Alex be here today?" asked Don.

"He's in town, and he knows about this. I wouldn't be surprised if he...ah, speak of the devil."

After exchanging greetings with Alex Overly, Don said, "I'm sorry you didn't make it to the show last night."

"I'm free tonight. You're playing, I suppose?"

"We are. Want to come? We'll save you a house seat."

"I'd like to, yes."

"One?"

"Yes, yes. Only one."

"It'll be at the box office for you," Don promised.

Gehring stepped from an inner office. "Gentlemen, please follow me." He led the men into a large office, and everyone seated themselves around a conference table.

"No one but us?" asked Mark.

"For the purposes of this meeting, no," Gehring said, putting on a pair of glasses. "I must tell you today's meeting is being held following a number of other meetings related to this will. I have read the pertinent documents. I have assured myself of the veracity of the documents. I can summarize them and make our meeting brief." He looked around the table, and no one suggested lengthening the meeting.

"Very well. Ms. Brunner left a fortune of just under eighty-seven million dollars. She has no immediate family. She's made a number of bequests to different friends—some three dozen of them—totaling some five million dollars. Those people are being notified. Some fifteen million dollars will be dispersed to various charities listed by Ms. Brunner in her will. The money will be shared equally by the charities involved. Another ten million dollars will be divided among twenty-seven different theatre groups in New York City and elsewhere. This amount will also be divided equally."

Gehring reached for a pitcher and poured himself a glass of water.

Don leaned over to Mark as Gehring drank his water. "Still fifty-seven million to go."

Mark quietly shushed him.

"The remaining money, nearly sixty-million dollars, is to be invested in Barset Enterprises. The profits from this investment have been signed over to Anthony Barset for reinvestment." Gehring stopped and took off his glasses. "Any questions?"

"Mr. Gehring," said Mark.

"Yes, Mr. Louis."

"Ashley gave fifty-seven million dollars to Mr. Barset?"

"As an investment, Mark," Barset explained. "She came around on the last day. She loved Illyria. You saw how she fell in love with it."

"She told me she was thinking of investing only a few million dollars with you."

"Originally, that's what she told me, too. I'd call her a shy investor. She'd never done anything like this before. Her husband, I'm sure, always handled that end of things, but after experiencing the island, she decided to invest the major share of her fortune in it."

"I have looked at the papers signed by Ms. Brunner," said Gehring. "They're dated the day of her death. The signature is without doubt hers. It is witnessed by Mr. Overly here. It is a legal change to the arrangements in her will. I must now set about liquidating Ms. Brunner's assets to accumulate the money necessary to satisfy the will and Mr. Barset."

"What about our theatre company?" asked Don.

"Ah, yes. I'm sorry." Gehring put his glasses back on. "She did write into her will that the amount of money residing in the AWB Theatre Company account would be used to operate the theatre for as long as the money lasted. Plus, you're one of the twenty-seven theatres companies mentioned in the will, so you'll get your share of that. I believe I can say Ms. Brunner hardly expected to meet her end on this recent trip. She no doubt expected to live for many more years, and sometime in the future would have planned something quite different for your company. The company meant a great deal to her."

"But her investment in Barset Enterprises is legal, correct, Mr. Gehring?" Barset put in, more as a demand than a question.

"As far as I am concerned, it is. The profits, however...I'm not certain you have absolute control over them, Mr. Barset."

"We've had this conversation already," Barset replied. "The language is clear. She signed the contract, and Mr. Overly witnessed it. I have discretion over the reinvestment of all profits to be made from the initial investment. I don't see any ambiguity."

Gehring, a man in his late fifties with a full head of gray hair, began to glow red in bright contrast to his hair color. He removed his glasses and tossed them on the table. "You may be right, but I believe more work needs to be done to make certain."

"Well, you do the work, and do your liquidating as quickly as you can. I'm planning to move on the Illyria project by spring."

Gehring turned back to Mark. "The theatre company has three hundred twenty-one thousand dollars in its account, plus whatever you'll receive from the will. Checks, you know, were signed by both Ms. Brunner and Barbara Gray, your business manager. Ms. Gray can continue to sign checks along with another member of the permanent company to be selected by the company. When you've decided who, please let me know, Mr. Louis, and I'll effect the necessary changes. Any questions?"

"I have none," said Barset. "Alex, you?"

Alex shook his head.

"We'll stay in touch, Mr. Gehring," said Barset. "You theatre people, everything clear?"

"I suppose so," said Don when Mark chose not to respond.

Barset rose. "Fine. Alex, I'll need you around three this afternoon at the hotel."

"I'll be there."

Barset extended his hand to Gehring. "I thank you for your time and effort, Mr. Gehring."

Gehring shook Barset's hand, neither nodding nor speaking.

Barset said good-bye and left the office.

"Have you folks had breakfast?" asked Alex.

"Just some juice at home," Don replied.

"Let's have breakfast then. My treat."

They bid farewell to Gehring and left the office.

Alex led Mark and Don to a corner restaurant on Lexington Avenue, two blocks from the lawyer's office. They settled into a booth, Don and Mark on one side.

"So, Ashley gave away the bulk of her fortune to Anthony Barset," Mark said after the waitress left with their order.

"'Gave away is a bit severe, don't you think?" Alex replied. "Ashley's change of mind is why I didn't take our prisoner to St.

Thomas. I stayed to witness her and Anthony conclude their business. She fell in love with the island, and Anthony would have made a great deal of money for her. No question. It's why the other investors are turning their money over to Anthony. He's made a lot of money for a lot of people in his time."

"And the bit about the profits?" Mark asked.

"She might have taken them out or reinvested them if she hadn't died. I don't know. She had plenty of other money to live on. I can't say I know what she envisioned. Maybe coming to live on Illyria part of the year once the hotel was built."

Mark nodded. "She did mention something like that to me. She thought it would be pleasant to have her own suite waiting for her anytime she wanted to fly down." He accepted his plate of eggs from the waitress, and the men ate in silence.

Finally, Alex said, "What will you folks do? How long will the theatre's account keep you going?"

"Through this season certainly," said Mark. "We'll have to talk about continuing into next season."

"I understand you live on the money you earn from the theatre."

"Some of us, the permanent actors do," said Don.

"If you want to continue, you'll have to change how you operate. Start fundraising."

"Or we can put on more plays," said Don. "It was Lawrence's idea we concentrate on one play at a time."

"How much money has Barset raised for this island resort project?" asked Mark.

"Approximately three hundred fifty, more or less."

"And almost sixty of it is Ashley's. Sounds like Ashley invested more than anyone else in this project."

"Only by a little. The other five who've come aboard have invested fifty million dollars each. Anthony insisted on that level. The rest of the money comes from him and me."

"I never got the impression from Ashley she wanted to make such a deep commitment," Mark repeated.

Alex shifted in his seat. "Turns out she changed her mind. She knew what the others were investing. Anthony and I explained everything to her and by the last day, she showed nothing but enthusiasm."

After a moment's quiet, Alex slid out of the booth. "You two have another coffee. I have a few things to do." He waved the waitress over. She came and handed him the check. He threw a ten-dollar tip on the table. "I'm sorry if you're disappointed with how things turned out."

"Not your fault," said Don. "Oh, by the way. Do you have the number of Barset's place on Illyria, the phone number?"

Alex smiled. "Nelly on your mind? Sure. Here." He motioned for Don to hand him a napkin. He wrote the number on it and handed it back. "This is it." He turned to leave.

Don called after him, "Don't forget *Twelfth Night*."

Alex turned. "I'll be there." He walked off.

"Did he seem to get progressively more uncomfortable during breakfast?" Mark asked his friend when Alex was gone.

"He did."

"Why?" Mark pocketed the napkin with Nelly's phone number.

"You tell me."

"Maybe something is rotten, and he knows where."

"You're back in *Hamlet* again. That was my line, not yours, though."

"More coffee?"

"Why not? We have the whole day to kill."

"You can come to my place later before we go to the theatre."

"Kristy there?"

"Yeah. I told her I might be bringing you home. She said she'd come up with a fancy pre-theatre brunch for us. Give Karen a call."

"Sounds good. And we can call Illyria later. Maybe from the theatre when the ladies are not around." Don motioned for the waitress, and the two young men brooded over their refilled cups of coffee.

~ * ~

Back in the tiny lobby office of the Bouwerie Lane Theatre, Don said, "I'll leave Alex a note along with the ticket. Maybe he'll want to meet us afterwards at Phebe's."

Mark handed Don a pen. "Do it, and hurry up before anybody else gets here. I want to make the call to Illyria."

Don tucked a note along with the ticket into an envelope and wrote "Alex Overly" on the outside. "There. Into the Will Call box."

Mark unfolded the napkin Alex had provided. "You want to dial? Nelly might respond better to you."

"Nobody dials anymore. What kind of wordsmith are you? You punch or tap or key in. Sure, I'll do it. Man, all these numbers." Don tapped in the requisite digits and waited. "It's ringing. Three. Four. Yes, hello. I'm calling from the United States. My name is Don Lovett. Who is this? Oh, Adiba. You remember me, good. I'm trying to reach Nelaneda. Is she there? I'll wait...he's getting her."

"Put me on after you say hello."

Don held up one finger. "Nelly, hi. This is Don. How are you? We're doing our play, right. It goes on in about three hours. I wish you were here, too."

Mark rolled his eyes and gave Don a hurry-up sign.

Don raised his finger again. "Listen, Nelly, besides calling because I miss you, I'm calling for another reason. You remember my friend, Mark?"

"Why wouldn't she remember me?"

Don waved his hand to quiet Mark. "He wants to talk to you about those murders. Yes. Here he is." Don handed the receiver to Mark. "Let me have it back before you hang up."

"Hello, Nelly. Nice to talk to you. You might be able to help me. Listen, I don't think those first three murders were committed by the man they flew to St. Thomas. Well, no. I can't say who committed the murders. I don't know who. I'm calling because I'm afraid Ashley's death the last day might not have been an accident. You can help by doing something for me. I read the reports, but I don't remember the dates when each of the murders occurred. You can find out? Good. Find out, too, whether Mr. Barset was on the island those days. Well, no, no. Don't be angry. I...no, I'm not asking you to be disloyal. Whatever you tell me will remain confidential. Yes, he's right here. She wants to talk to you." Mark handed the phone back to Don.

"Yes, it's Don, Nelly. No, I don't. Yes, it's only a question of where Mr. Barset...okay. Okay. Sure. No, of course we're not accusing Mr. Barset of anything." Don looked at Mark and sighed as he listened to Nelly. "I understand, Nelly. Okay. Can I call you again? Yes. Bye."

"So?"

"She said I can call again, for whatever it's worth. I never thought you'd point a finger at Barset."

Mark tucked the phone number back into his wallet. "It did get a reaction, didn't it?"

"Why would Barset be killing natives when he's hoping to build a resort there?"

The phone rang. Mark and Don looked at one another.

Don said, "If Nelly called Barset, and he's calling us, I'm going to find another deserted island to flee to."

"Pick it up."

Don lifted the receiver and handed it to Mark. Mark grimaced and pushed the phone back to Don.

"Hello. Yes, speaking. I'll hold. Molly Frederick's office," he said to Mark, his eyebrows lifting.

Mark gave a thumbs up and left the office, closing the door behind him. He didn't know why he'd been so abrupt with Nelly. He'd wanted to ask her whether she'd heard anything about the man they'd taken to St. Thomas, or whether she'd heard anything from the native people about the murders, especially Ashley's, but instead he'd jumped right to Barset. No wonder she bristled. He'd handled it badly and found out nothing.

Mark tried to recapture Nelly's voice, looking for the tiniest hint of fear, a sense she knew something but was afraid to mention it. He sat in an aisle seat. Her reaction had not eliminated the possibility, but after this debacle, any future conversation with her would be problematic.

He heard the office door open and close behind him. Don came down the aisle.

"She wants me to test for a movie part on Monday. Am I available? Am I available? It's not a small part either. More a medium one, she said. This is…I can't believe it."

"Where do you have to go?"

"Someplace in Queens. I wrote the address down."

Mark shook Don's hand. "Well, good luck. I'm afraid we're going to lose you soon, my friend."

"Well, your loss is Hollywood's gain. Imagine. A movie—for money! No more Park Slope."

"House in Hollywood, vacations in Illyria. Pretty soon you'll be rich enough for us to hit you up for a donation to keep the AWB Theatre Company going."

"Now you're getting into the spirit," Don said, laughing. "You know what should happen, though?"

"Tell me."

"You should run the company."

"Think so?"

"Sure. If you don't, who will?"

Always looking for something new to keep himself occupied, the thought had already crossed Mark's mind. He'd told Kristy he wanted to talk to her when they found some time, and this was the topic he planned to raise. He would like to run the theatre while the money lasted. Why not add another trade to his jack-of-all, master-of-none list?

"While we're talking about the theatre," Mark said, "I thought I'd tell the group about the will and suggest a meeting tomorrow before the performance to settle the question of who signs the checks."

"It's got to be you. I'll speak up for you."

"Thanks. Now, about Nelly. How did she sound to you?"

"Scared."

The tiny hairs on the back of Mark's neck rose. "Why do you say that?"

"That's how she sounded. Her outrage seemed a little forced."

"I wish I knew what she really thought."

Don raised a patient hand. "Give it a few days. Let me call back on my own when Bulldog Drummond isn't around to charm her. We did have the meager beginnings of a relationship going, you know."

"I'd advise you to call when Karen isn't around."

"That you didn't have to tell me. I can call from the theatre, right?"

"Sure. I'll be signing the checks, remember?"

"What do you think of this whole Barset situation?"

"A bit smelly?"

Don tipped his head to the side in doubt. "But Barset's story is credible. Ashley did fall in love with the island. She did sign the papers."

"Whoever did this to Ashley will have slipped up somewhere."

"*If* somebody did this to Ashley. You're the only one to think it might not have been an accident."

"Yes, well. Let's put that aside for now. We do have a play to put on. Feel like it?"

"Yes, I do. You bet I do."

Mark rose. "Then let's get downstairs." He preceded Don down the aisle. The two men leaped the foot and a half onto the stage and disappeared behind the scenes.

~ * ~

Alex Overly had a table for five prepared with a bottle of red wine and a bottle of white wine already uncorked when the four actors arrived at Phebe's. When Mark caught his eye, Alex waved the group over.

Don greeted him. "Alex, I'm glad you hung around. Did you enjoy the performance?"

"I didn't want anyone to have to wait for a drink. Everyone, choose your favorite color." He poured the wine and toasted the actors with his Scotch. "Order some food. You're my guests." He motioned the waiter over. "To answer your question, yes, I enjoyed the play immensely. I wish I had the talent to do what you people can do."

"Act?" asked Mark.

"Yes, act. It must be wonderful to have that language inside of you and play the little games Shakespeare prepared for you." He lifted his glass and drained it. He motioned the waiter again and ordered another Johnny Walker Black.

Don said, "The company met today before the performance—about Ashley's will."

"*Ah*, yes. How did the company respond?"

Mark answered. "We're lucky the account has as much money in it as it does. Plus we'll get the extra coming in from the will. If the cupboard had been bare, we'd have been out of business."

"I'm glad to hear you'll be good for a while," said Alex.

Don added, "We at this table hope Mark puts himself forward as the person to keep the theatre together."

"You don't think Marty will want it, do you?" asked Kristy.

"He's not even a permanent member," Don pointed out.

"And even if he does, no doubt only permanent members of the troupe, of whom there are five, will vote. I count four votes right here."

Alex laughed. "I hope for your sake, Mark, the vote isn't three-two."

Everyone laughed along.

The food arrived, and the conversation flowed. Everyone ate heartily except for Alex, who picked at his dinner. After Alex ordered a second bottle of red wine—Kristy and Karen were still working on the white—and another Scotch for himself, Mark put a question to him.

"Alex, how did Ashley seem that final day? You stayed behind, didn't fly off to St. Thomas, and spent some of the day with her."

Alex spread his hands. "You saw her in the morning. Didn't she take a walk and miss breakfast? Illyria enchanted her. She said so repeatedly. She said she was glad we'd captured the murderer so she could walk about safely in the time..."

"In the time what?" asked Kristy.

"...in the time she had left on the island."

"Irony, eh?" said Mark to a silent table.

"At any rate," Alex continued, "she wanted to be part of Anthony's plans for the island."

"To the tune of practically her whole fortune?" asked Mark. "When she talked to me of being a minor investor?"

"You keep bringing this up, Mark. I don't know what she told you about being a minor investor. At the beginning, I'm sure she did consider herself a minor investor, but you heard—by the end of her stay, she'd raised her investment considerably."

"She dismissed her investment to me as being of no consequence. She and I joked about it." Mark watched Alex lift his glass to his lips. Their eyes met but briefly. Mark lifted his glass and drank.

"What can I tell you?" Alex downed his Scotch. "She changed her mind."

Quiet descended on the table until Don came to the rescue. "Had you ever seen *Twelfth Night* before?"

Alex looked down into his empty glass before answering. "No. No, this was my first time." He looked at his watch and stood. "I have to get back to the hotel. I want to talk to Anthony before he goes to sleep. Enjoy the rest of your evening. I'll take care of the check on the way out." He turned away and, after conducting business with the waiter, left the restaurant.

Don filled his and Mark's glasses. "Why do I get the impression whenever you and Alex talk, twelve other things are going on at the same time? Why did he leave so fast?"

"Discomfort? You tell me. Remember when Lawrence was killed, and we went over every little detail trying to piece things together, I had a feeling we lacked one tiny piece and the piece, once found, would bring the picture clear."

"And now?" said Kristy.

"The way things have worked out—especially with the will—it's easy to imagine some intelligence behind this. Easy to imagine this being the result of some plan."

"How could it be?" asked Karen. "Random killings on Illyria. Ashley falling to her death. What plan? Ashley's death was an accident. There doesn't need to be a plan to produce an accident."

"Yes," said Kristy, "but if the accident was a murder, as Mark thinks, it had to be planned, and if so, the next question is— how much of everything was planned? Our trip to Illyria? The random murders? Ashley's murder? The will?"

She looked at Mark. They all did.

He laughed. "Murder Solutions for four hundred? I don't know, but I do know this. My instinct tells me to keep digging. People we talk to about the murder react strangely—Alex, Nelly."

"You talked to Nelly?" asked Karen.

"I called her from the theatre," Mark answered. "She got upset and wouldn't tell me anything. Let's put any talk of Illyria aside for now and give it some independent thought on our own time. Four heads are better than one. All agree?"

Without dissent, their night went on.

Ten

Kristy had gone back to her own apartment for a day or two to attend to certain chores, leaving Mark alone. He got some orange juice from his decrepit refrigerator and sat at his tiny dining table in his tiny apartment. Like his refrigerator, his neighborhood was decrepit, but reputedly on the rise, boasting a few new restaurants and a sparkling new six-story brick apartment building on the same block as his own. Mark knew Kristy didn't much like staying in his rundown place, but she did so anyway four or five nights a week. He'd visited her shared-by-three-others two-bedroom apartment in Chelsea. If they wanted privacy, his apartment was the only choice.

Mark looked again at the blurry photographs he'd rescued from Ashley's camera. Maybe Nelly would succeed where he and Kristy had failed and be able to find a native who'd taken the photograph. If she did, Ashley's fall might have been an accident after all.

Mark opened a pastry box and broke off a piece of fat-free breakfast cake Kristy had provided. He couldn't talk about Ashley to Barset, that cut-your-throat-for-a-dollar businessman. If he talked to

Alex with no one else around, he might learn something. Alex had reacted yesterday to Mark's response, "Act?" after Alex had said, "I wish I could do what you people can do." The barb of Mark's retort had stuck. Alex Overly was acting, but why? What did it mean?

He'd need to be face to face with Alex to judge his reactions. From the dining table, he looked at the bedside clock, thinking one-room apartments, with everything in clear view, did have their conveniences. 9:15, it read. He had nothing to do today. Alex and Barset were closeted at the Waldorf Astoria with some of the investors. Could a visit to the Waldorf hurt?

He couldn't see how. What the hell, he thought? What was there to lose?

An hour later, he stood before the front desk of the Waldorf and spoke to the desk clerk.

"Yes, Alex Overly. I'd like to call up to him. I don't have the room number,"

The clerk smiled politely. "One moment, sir." He tapped a few times on his computer keyboard. "Mr. Overly has checked out."

"When?"

"This morning, sir."

"How about Mr. Barset? Anthony Barset. He and Mr. Overly are partners. Is he still here? I can talk to him."

"Let me check. Yes, Mr. Barset is still with us. Pick up the yellow phone, and I'll connect you with his room."

When someone picked up, Mark said, "Mr. Barset, please. This is Mark Louis from the AWB Theatre Company. Mr. Barset knows me. We're friends. I'll wait."

A moment later Barset came on the line, loud as ever. "Mark, how are you? What can I do for you?"

"I'm downstairs. I owed Alex a breakfast, and I thought he'd be here, but they tell me he checked out."

"Yes, he has. He flew back to Illyria this morning. Sorry you missed him."

"When will he be back?"

"Hard to say. We're planning to move ahead quickly, and I need Alex down there."

"I'm sorry I missed him, too."

"I'm here with a few of my investors, and I have to get back to them, but if there's anything I can do…"

"No, there's nothing. Thanks."

Mark left the hotel and stepped into a gloomy, cold day with a threat of snow in the stillness of the air. He walked toward the subway. It would be difficult to call and talk to Nelly if Alex were there—not that Nelly had been much help anyway—but if he meant to try again, he needed to make the call before Alex arrived. It meant he needed Don, who would have to call her today, right now, but Don had gone to Queens for his screen test. Mark took out his cell phone and left a message for him to call as soon as possible.

Finally, at twelve-thirty, Don responded to his message.

"How'd your reading go?" Mark asked.

"They'll let me know. A 'don't call me; I'll call you' kind of thing. But I did okay. I had to read a scene from the movie they're planning to make. Love, murder, sex—the usual. Cute actress reading back at me. I hope she gets the part. What's up?"

"Overly left for Illyria this morning."

"*Hmmm.* He didn't mention anything to us, did he?"

"No, and I figure if he's in the house down there, it's going to be difficult to talk to Nelly without him and Barset getting wind. Can you call Nelly now, right away, before Alex has time to get to the house?"

"He's got to go to St. Thomas first. We have time. Shall I meet you at the theatre?"

"Yeah, I'll go now."

"Okay. On my way."

When Don arrived, Mark handed him a list of things he wanted him to ask Nelly.

"Kind of repeat everything like you're having trouble hearing her," Mark suggested.

"Then I'll get an idea of what she's saying."

Don tapped in the necessary numbers and waited. "Hello. Hello. Nelly?"

He bobbed his head once at Mark.

"It's Don. How are you? You were hoping I'd call? Well, I'm glad I did." Don laughed. "I agree. It would be nice to have you feeding me again."

Mark rolled his eyes and tapped the paper where he'd written his questions.

"Sometime soon, I hope. But listen, I'm sort of concerned about what happened on the island when I visited. Yes, to my friend, Ashley."

From Don's side of the conversation, Mark could tell the people on the island were still frightened because they didn't know what to make of Ashley's death. No, Nelly hadn't heard of any native taking a photograph of her, but she promised to continue asking around.

Don looked at Mark and grimaced. Now, the list moved to questions about Barset, and Don moved ahead cautiously. Nelly reported that Barset was on the island for all of the murders except the second one. She remembered calling Barset at his New York office to tell him about it. She had heard nothing about the disposition of the case against the man they'd taken to St. Thomas.

"Did you know Alex is on his way?" asked Don. "You expect him around two o'clock? It's almost two now."

Mark scribbled a note and handed it to Don, who glanced at it and passed the request along to Nelly.

"There you have it," said Don after he'd hung up. "She seemed much more composed this time."

"She promised to ask around about someone taking Ashley's picture?"

"Yes."

"And she'll call here next Monday collect?" This was the request he'd passed to Don.

"She said she would. Two o'clock, just as you asked. Now what?"

"We wait, I suppose."

"I have to get over to Karen's. I promised to help her paint her bathroom today. I'm staying with her until we go back to work on Thursday."

Mark stood. "Thanks for coming right over."

"My pleasure. A chance to call Nelly and at your expense—a win-win situation."

"Coming into Phebe's any night?"

"I don't think so. I'll be covered with paint."

On the walk back to his apartment, Mark thought of another person who might be worth talking to. He fished around in this top dresser drawer for the card Mr. Gehring had given him during the investigation into Lawrence's murder. He found the card and made the call. The secretary took his name, number, and the fact that the call referred to Ashley's will and promised Gehring would return the call.

Mark threw himself onto his bed and clasped his hands behind his head. He and Kristy planned to meet at Phebe's around seven. Until then—for as long as it made sense to do it—he'd go over everything that had happened and search for the elusive one piece that might prove to be the key to unlocking the whole problem.

Eleven

Alex Overly eased the small plane toward a landing, and the beautiful island of Illyria, a portrait in green and gold, floated up toward him. Carlos was visiting for a few days in St. Thomas and had left the plane for him. Barset wanted him out of the country, away from where anyone asked questions. Fine. Barset didn't trust him? He'd deal with it. Barset didn't think him strong enough? It didn't matter. Better here in Illyria than New York, no matter what the reason. He tried to smile at the thought of Barset working away back in New York while he kept out of the way in sunny Illyria, but it wouldn't come.

The wheels touched down, and the plane rolled to a stop. Try as he might to ignore it, Barset's offhanded banishment rankled him. He'd been putting up with the great man's disdain and growing lack of confidence in him for a very long time, but it hadn't gotten any easier to digest.

"Screw him," Alex mumbled as he opened the cockpit door and climbed down to the ground. The heat felt wonderful.

"Hello, Alex," came a dreamy voice.

He turned. Nelly leaned against a jeep. They walked toward each other and embraced.

"I'm glad you have come alone," said Nelly. "So glad." She kissed him, and he ran his hands along her hips, feeling the contours he knew so well.

Resentment aside, Barset had done him a favor—not that he realized it—sending him back here. A great favor.

They stepped away from one another.

"Those young men, the actors, have called twice. The last time, an hour ago."

Alex frowned. "I knew they would. They asked me for your number. What did they want?"

"Mark called first. He does not think the strange man they captured did those killings, and he doesn't think the old woman's death was an accident."

"Is that a fact?"

"He asked whether Mr. Barset was on the island during the times of the killings."

"He's worried about Barset, is he? Okay."

"His call frightened me. I told him I would not talk about Mr. Barset. It would be disloyal of me."

Alex ran a hand through his hair. "He really thinks the Brunner woman was murdered?"

"Today, the other one called—Don, the one who likes me." Nelly made a demure face.

"Yes, you're very likable. It would be a good thing right now to keep him liking you. What did he want?"

"I told him Mr. Barset was off the island for the second murder. Do you recall?"

"Yes, I recall."

"Then he wanted to know about the man Carlos flew to St. Thomas."

Alex walked to the jeep and put his bag in the backseat. "Him? He'll be locked up forever. Crazy as a loon. I checked on him when we touched down there. They can't find out where he came from or even who he is. He keeps talking about his orders from God."

"That is good then?" Nelly asked after she'd climbed behind the wheel.

"I suppose."

"Do I tell Don about him? He wants me to call him next Monday and reverse the charges. He does not want you or Mr. Barset to know."

"Very cunning. Sure, you can say I mentioned it to you."

"What else shall I tell him?"

"I imagine you can figure out what to tell him on your own."

"You do trust me then."

"Do I have much choice? Start the car."

"That's not the answer I want to hear. Let's go back to the house. We will get undressed, and I will ask you again." She tossed her hair, started the engine, and drove away.

~ * ~

Mr. Gehring couldn't find time for Mark until Thursday morning at nine o'clock, an early beginning to the day for Mark. The secretary told Mark to go right in. He entered an office smaller than the room in which the will had been read, where he found Gehring seated behind a desk.

The lawyer rose and shook Mark's hand. "Mr. Louis, please sit."

Mark chose one of the two red, high-backed leather chairs facing Gehring's desk. The lawyer's desk was large, made of glistening dark wood, and impeccably neat.

"I'm told you've come to talk to me about Ashley," said Gehring.

"I have." Mark cleared his throat. "I believe someone pushed Ashley to her death on the island. The way things have transpired indicate, to me, a series of events that haven't occurred randomly." Mark had practiced those two sentences fifty times on the subway ride uptown. He wanted to sound intelligent, and he wanted Gehring's attention.

Gehring's face congealed into a morass of stern lines. "Do you realize what you're saying, young man?"

Mark reached into his jacket pocket and withdrew the photos. "When Ashley left the house her last day on the island, she carried a camera. I found the wrecked camera near the rocks where Ashley fell. I managed to get these photos out of it."

Gehring gave Mark a hard look before pulling the photographs across his desk. He inspected them slowly, one by one. He looked up at Mark puzzled. "What is it you imply they show?"

"We can agree, can't we, even though the pictures are clouded, the person in this picture..." Mark leaned forward and tapped a photograph. "...is Ashley. My friends agree with me. It's the final photo taken that day."

Gehring rose and took the photograph to the window. He studied it and then nodded. "It seems to be Ashley. And your point?"

"She's standing on the spot from which she fell."

Gehring walked back to his desk and sat. His eyes went from Mark to the photo and back to Mark again. "I'll have to take your word for that, but I see what you're getting at. Someone took this picture."

"Exactly."

"So someone was with Ashley at the exact spot where she fell on the day she fell."

"More than that. I'm suggesting whoever took the photograph might have pushed Ashley to her death."

Gehring's mouth pursed. "Quite a leap you're making. Anyone could have happened by to take her picture."

"No, you haven't been to this island, Illyria. It is unlikely anyone would have been walking where Ashley fell. She wandered around by herself, well off the beaten track—and even the beaten track in Illyria is pretty desolate. No native has admitted taking Ashley's picture, and, believe me, we've asked around. But we're still looking into it." Nelly crossed Mark's mind as he and Gehring studied each other.

Gehring had achieved the thickness of middle age but appeared healthy and vigorous. Sighing, he removed his glasses. "Why have you come to me?"

"I connect Ashley's death with the unexpected outcome of her will."

"And thus with Barset?"

"And thus with Barset. There was, as you know, a ton of money involved."

Gehring ran his left hand through his gray hair. "You are audacious if nothing else, Mr. Louis. I admit, the will surprised me. Not so much the will, but the contract Mr. Barset brought forward changing the will. It's as legal as anything I see every day."

"Fortuitous timing, wasn't it?"

"Extremely."

"Would professional ethics allow you to talk to me about Ashley and Barset? Their common history? Were you Mr. Brunner's lawyer when he and Barset did business? I know it was some time ago."

"I represented Wellington for years, going back long before he met Ashley or Anthony Barset. Yes, with both Ashley and Wellington dead, there's no reason I shouldn't talk to you about this. I would like to."

The office intercom buzzed.

Gehring tapped the necessary button. "Yes?"

"Mrs. Apfelbaum is here about the divorce settlement."

"Thanks. Mr. Louis, let's make an appointment."

"Do you have the Brunner records in your office?"

"I have what involved me, but Well would have kept a more complete set of records in his office in his apartment. I don't believe Ashley would ever dispose of them. She never said she did. Besides, I don't think she'd even know what they were. I'm fairly certain they're still there. Why don't we meet at Ashley's apartment? I have the keys." He reached for his appointment book and opened it. "I believe you'll be busy the next few nights with your play, and I'll be busy days. How about Sunday night?"

"The play ends Sunday around five."

"So, shall we say six, a little after?"

"I'll be there."

Both men rose, and Gehring came around his desk to shake Mark's hand again.

"I'm looking forward to an interesting conversation, Mr. Gehring."

"I'm afraid you may be right, Mr. Louis."

~ * ~

When the play ended Sunday afternoon, Mark quickly changed out of costume, eager to keep his appointment with Gehring. His selection as managing director for the theatre company had been unanimous, and his new duties in the theatre had kept his mind occupied for the past four days, but now he would put the theatre business and fantasy world of Illyria aside for a few hours in the interest of looking into what happened on the true-life island of Illyria.

"I'll be waiting for you at your apartment," were the last words Kristy said to him as he hurried out the basement door of the theatre.

Forty minutes later, Mark sought admittance from the doorman of Ashley's apartment building.

"Go right up." The doorman picked up a telephone to announce Mark's arrival.

Ashley had lived at Sixtieth and Park Avenue in a luxurious nine-room apartment. No doubt this apartment would be one of the assets Gehring would liquidate to furnish Barset with his investment money.

Gehring waited for him by the open apartment door, dressed casually in tan slacks, socks to match, and loafers. His shirt was silk, long-sleeved, and a rich blue. The gray of his hair shone in contrast to the deep blue of his shirt. If he'd worked a bit to get rid of the slight paunch he carried, he'd give Alex Overly a run for his money as far as looks went.

"I can't say I mind much hanging out in Ashley's apartment," said Gehring, closing the door and leading Mark into the living room. "I consider my apartment a pretty large one—three bedrooms in a pre-war building on the Upper West Side—but it doesn't compare to this place."

"My apartment on Avenue B would fit into one of Ashley's bathrooms," said Mark. He removed his jacket and tossed it onto a chair.

"Would you like a drink?" Gehring indicated his own drink sitting on a coffee table surrounded by the three red leather sofas forming a

U before the fireplace. "I'm having Scotch—my first. Ashley has some fine Scotch. One of her assets I refuse to sell."

"I think I will have a Scotch. It's not what I usually drink, but this isn't where I usually drink." He was beginning to like Gehring. It pleased him, since he might very well need his help later.

Gehring went to the bar in the corner of the room and returned with a solid-looking short glass one-third full of liquid gold. It had no ice.

"I'm not assuming you wouldn't know the name of this Scotch..." Gehring began slowly, handing the glass to Mark.

"You may assume," said Mark, taking the glass.

"...but it's Dalwhinnie, a single-malt, very delicious. I will refuse to the death to allow you to put an ice cube in it."

As Mark sipped, the dusky flavor rose up inside of him and seemed to fill his head.

"Do you like it?" Gehring asked, sitting and picking up his own drink.

"Wow! This is not what I'm used to."

"Enjoy it, and more after it. Let's talk. I recall what you did when Lawrence was killed. I know I can place my confidence in you, as Ashley did."

"Can you tell me about the relationship between Ashley and Barset?"

"As I said, I was Wellington's attorney. Well was a wheeler-dealer of real charm. He brokered deals for others and took a healthy commission. Then Barset happened along. Barset wanted Well to help him raise money for a computer venture—Q1 Computers, I believe—made abroad, inexpensive but seemingly reliable. What I also recall is Barset putting a little too much information, a little too much control, into Well's hands. Wellington knew how big this Q1 could be, so he raised money on his own and worked the deal in a way that cut Barset out of the whole thing. As a sop, he left Barset a software importing scheme of some kind, expensive to initiate. It didn't go over at all, and Barset lost his stake. Q1, on the other hand, went through the roof for five or six years. Well made millions on top of the millions he'd already made. Barset had to go back and start over from the beginning."

"Where was Ashley when this went on?"

"Well courted her during the Barset venture. He sort of bragged about the big deal he had put together as a tactic to impress Ashley. I remember a rugged two-week period where the whole situation hung fire. Barset caught on Well had left him the ragged part of the cloth, and he struggled to get in on the Q1 piece of the deal. Well fought hard to keep him out. Everything fell Wellington's way, though, and he married Ashley not only to celebrate their relationship but to celebrate the successful...and lucrative...deal."

"You were present for this?"

"Oh yes. I got out those records." He indicated the pile of folders on the coffee table. "I looked through them while I waited. I've been here since four-thirty."

"Did the two men socialize during this time?"

"Oh, yes. We had meetings here at this apartment, cocktail parties with other interested investors. Something, I'm sure, like what you saw on Illyria. Ashley would have been at the social occasions."

"How bad were the feelings that came out of it all?"

"When the intense period of wheeling and dealing ended—after the wicked two weeks I mentioned—Barset knew he'd lost and seemed oddly calm. I remember him congratulating Wellington on his shrewdness and saying he'd learned a lot from him. He rose and left the meeting."

"Would Ashley have been at the meeting?"

"No, no."

"And the wedding? Did Barset attend?"

Gehring paused. "I can't recall, but not likely. If he did, he made no impression on me."

"So now he gets back the money he lost on this Q1 thing plus a nice addition to it."

"So it would seem." Gehring drained his glass and went to the bar for a refill.

Mark took a quick look through the stack of papers on the coffee table.

Gehring returned and sat. "You are the only person with the temerity to voice the slightest concern that coincidence isn't governing things here."

"What's happening to Ashley's money right now?"

"I've already given Barset what's available, and I'm working to raise the rest. I'll put this apartment up for sale as soon as possible."

"And the profits from the investment?"

"The profits are a question worth going to court over, but, of course, someone must file suit. There's no next of kin. There are the charities and the theatres, of course, but the way she left the will makes that difficult."

"But you're looking into it?"

"If something can be done, I will do it. Well didn't like Barset from the get-go. I don't like him either."

"Neither do I." Mark sipped from his glass. "Can I file suit on behalf of AWB?"

"Can the theatre file suit?" Gehring shrugged. "The theatre might be best positioned to bring suit. Ashley was deeply involved in it—worked there, had a reputation in theatre. How she chose those charities is beyond me. I think, depending on what she read in *The Times* on any particular day, she jotted down the name of a charity. I don't see any of them bringing suit. I can't say right now."

"You'll find out?"

"Yes, yes, I will. Another?"

Mark handed Gehring his glass and the lawyer went to refill it.

"Thanks," Mark said, taking the glass, again a third full of shimmering gold. "If I need a little money to look into this, will I cause a problem if I use the theatre's money?" Mark explained his new role in the theatre. "It wouldn't be much—so far, only phone calls to Illyria."

"I promise not to complain. Talk to me if anything serious, moneywise, comes up."

"And if I need to talk to you about anything else?"

"Call any time. Leave a message if I'm not available." Gehring sipped. "Has any of this conversation helped you? Any investigatory insights? I admit I don't like the way things have worked out."

"Clearly Barset has turned the tables on the Brunner fortune. He's gotten even, if that's what he intended to do. May I take these papers home? Just what are they?"

"Notes of meetings kept by me or by Well. Letters back and forth between the two parties. The narrative is pretty straightforward. The file's in good order. I'll need it back, though."

"Sure. How about Alex Overly? I mean, back then."

"He was around, but I don't think he and Barset had partnered up yet. I don't know much about him."

"Can you find out about him?"

"I can try, yes. Anything else?"

"No, no. Nothing right now."

"Then let's sit back, finish our second drinks, maybe have a third, and be off. My wife expects me home for dinner. Sometimes she complains about my coming home smelling of alcohol. I do often unwind a bit before I go home. She doesn't drink much herself, glass of wine, maybe. Know what I do?"

Mark shook his head.

"Soon as I get home, I make myself a short Scotch on the rocks. It covers the lingering aroma of..." Gehring lifted his glass. Mark gave a brief laugh. "I'll file that for future reference."

"To the soft and happy world of alcohol—a pleasant place to visit." He and Mark touched glasses, then sat back.

~ * ~

Mark went out on Monday to buy a bottle of Dalwhinnie to share with Don after they took Nelly's call, but when he found the Scotch section in Astor Wines and Spirits and saw Dalwhinnie priced at seventy-two dollars a bottle, he changed his mind. A 1.75 liter bottle of Frontera cabernet found its way to the register instead.

"I almost bought you some good booze for later," Mark said as Don tossed his coat on the small desk in the Bouwerie Lane Theatre office. "A little out of my price range, though."

"So what did you get? Ah, I see. Our perennial favorite—whatever's on sale. Nine bucks, right? Bought a bottle myself last week at Astor."

"Did you hear anything yet about your trip to Hollywood?"

"No, no. I'm not obsessing over it. If it happens, it happens."

"Good philosophy. Want some wine now? It's only one-thirty. We have half an hour. I already got a couple of paper cups."

The phone rang and ended talk of a drink.

Mark looked at his watch. "She's a half-hour early, if it's her. You answer it."

Don picked up. "Hello. Yes, it is. Yes, I'll accept the charges. Nelly, hi, how are you? Nice to hear your voice, too."

As Mark listened, he wrote down some questions he wanted Don to ask and passed them to him.

From the conversation, Mark gleaned that Alex had gone out for a walk, and so the early call. He learned the arrested man was still in St. Thomas. No one had been found who had taken Ashley's picture. She confirmed again that Barset was off the island when the second murder occurred. Alex Overly was not on the island when the first murder happened. When Ashley died, he was working upstairs.

After a round of flirting, Mark gave Don a punch and rubbed the thumb and fingers of his right hand together. He had Don ask Nelly to promise that if she found out anything new, she would call the theatre—collect—and leave a message for Don to get in touch with her. Don and Nelly parted tenderly.

"So," Mark asked, "anything other than what I heard?"

"Overly told her he checked on the crazy man, and he'll probably be locked up forever. You heard about the photograph, right? Nothing there. What else? Overly's busy working every day. Nelly said she hardly gets to see him except when she puts his meals on the table. Oh, and she misses me."

"I heard that part—more often than I care to remember."

"She promised to call again if she learned something new. I don't know how she can find out anything, though."

"We may get lucky. You want to hang around a while? I met with Gehring last night at Ashley's."

"Ah, I see where the sudden urge for quality whiskey comes from. You gonna open that bottle?"

Mark took a corkscrew from the bottom drawer of the desk. "Yeah, we were both blotto when we left there. Drinking fancy Scotch. We were going to stop after the third drink, but he snuck a short fourth in on us. I didn't complain. I felt it this morning, though."

"Where's Kristy?"

"Shopping. I'm meeting her in Phebe's at seven. How much you want?" Mark poured until Don tapped his hand.

"That'll be enough for now. Sure, I'll hang around. I hate making this trip to Manhattan and turning right around."

"Where's Karen?" Mark poured himself a half glass of wine.

"At home. I'll call and invite her in."

"Good. Gehring gave me a bunch of papers from Ashley's apartment. I have them at home. You can go over them with me while we sip on some of this fine wine."

"What kind of papers?"

"Ashley's husband's dealings with Barset."

"There's a clue somewhere in the pile?"

"You never know."

"Okay, let me call Karen. Then we'll go to your place and look for the needle in the haystack."

"Let's finish our wine first while I tell you what Gehring told me."

~ * ~

"So we spent over an hour looking through this enormous stack of papers the lawyer gave Mark," Don explained to Karen and Kristy at their table in Phebe's. "I didn't quite follow the drift exactly, could you, Mark?"

"Enough to see how Ashley's husband-to-be took the meat and left Barset the bone."

"And..." Kristy questioned.

"Well, it confirms what Gehring told me and what we've told you. Food's here."

After cutting her first strip of London broil, Karen asked, "Could that be a motive for Barset to grab as much of Ashley's money as possible? And kill her besides?"

"Think about it. The way things played out was the only way he'd get to keep her money and do what he wanted with it now, and likely in the future."

"You'll need more than that to make a case," said Kristy. "Don't give me that look. I know you don't like being told that, but it's true."

They ate in silence for a time.

"When we finish," said Karen, "why don't we start from the beginning and go step by step?"

"Mark and I did that walking over here," said Don.

Karen smiled. "How thorough could that have been? Two men talking."

"It's a good idea, Karen. We'll confer after dinner," insisted Kristy. "Pour some wine please, Mark."

During dinner, Mark listened to Kristy tell Karen about the shopping she'd done, and with Ashley's money on his mind, he wondered where Kristy's money came from. She seemed to spend much more than AWB's stipend provided her.

After the waiter cleared the table of their dinner debris, Mark started in. "First of all, the four natives were killed, the fourth by the lunatic they flew off to St. Thomas. He's still there. They can't find out who he is or where he's from."

"How do you know?" asked Karen.

"I told you before. I talked to Nelly. I got her number from Alex, and we've spoken a few times. I hoped she could help us out, and she promises to, but so far, she hasn't very much."

"Go on." Kristy readjusted her chair. "You lead."

"Yes, well, from what Nelly told us...me...Barset was on the island for the first and third murders, but not the second one."

"So who else could have been on the island?" asked Kristy.

"Alex, Nelly, Adiba, the three guards?" said Don.

"Everyone but Alex and Barset should have been on the island for all the murders," said Mark. "Nelly said Alex was missing when the first murder took place and there for the second and third. The others you mentioned must have been there—they live on the island."

"They have no reason to go around killing natives, do they? Or killing Ashley?" said Karen.

"No reason any of us can see, I'm sure," Mark agreed.

"The only thing we have...you have, suggesting Ashley was murdered is the blurry photograph," said Kristy.

"And the story Gehring told me."

"Mark," Kristy argued, "anyone might have taken the photograph of Ashley and at any time, and business deals get nasty all over New York every day, I'm sure."

"She was standing right at the spot she fell from."

"It doesn't mean she couldn't have stood there, gone for a walk, and come back later," Kristy countered.

Mark did not want to argue, since Kristy could be right. "Maybe after Lawrence, I have murder on the brain. It isn't likely both Ashley and Lawrence would be murdered within a few months of each other, is it?" His question got no response, so he went on. "Do you remember how we sat here like this when we noticed the out-of-work actor who turned out to be the key to Lawrence's murder? We saw him, asked the right questions, took the lucky path, and, bingo! The missing piece fell out of the sky."

"And you're hoping the sky will open again?" asked Kristy.

"If it doesn't, I'm going to have a hard time accepting this recent chain of events."

"None of us knows what to look for," said Don.

"We didn't last time, either," Mark reminded him. "But when it fell into our laps, we recognized it."

"You recognized it," said Don.

"And I'll recognize it again. Don't you worry. When it comes, I'll recognize it."

Twelve

Mark spent the next few days in his apartment with Kristy. The weather had turned gray, wet, and cold. Neither he nor Kristy had much desire to go out, and ate in each night. They made love. They read. They watched a little TV. And they talked over the series of events leading to Ashley's death. They'd argued, once heatedly, over what sense it made for anyone on the island to kill her. They left for the theatre Thursday afternoon no nearer agreement and continued the discussion as they walked.

"It's so slim a chance someone murdered her," argued Kristy. "Everyone is accounted for."

Mark listened. Maybe this time Kristy could convince him. "We know what time Barset and Haniel dropped Ashley off—twelve-fifteen. They were back at the house at twelve-twenty or so—together. Remember, we were about to have sandwiches? Barset was at the house when she died. The photo and Gehring's story aren't cause enough for you to spend so much time looking for a murderer."

"What about Alex?"

Kristy stopped and looked at him. She started up again and said, "You can't be serious. He, Barset, and Nelly agree he was upstairs when it happened. And only Barset, according to the theory you've... may I say concocted?"

"Why not? You've called it worse."

"Only Barset had a motive for harming Ashley. Not Alex. Barset. He got her to sign the contract investing her money, and then, according to you, to be certain the money stayed with him, to be certain she didn't change her mind, he killed her. All part of a revenge plot. It could make sense. There's a logic to it. I wouldn't put it past Barset, the little I know of him, but he wasn't there, and the others on the island are too far outside your theory to be involved. The other possibility is for some unknown person for some unknown reason to have pushed Ashley onto the rock."

They paused to wait for the light to change.

"Some unknown person killed three natives on the island for unknown reasons," said Mark.

"But he is sitting in jail in St. Thomas."

Mark shook his head. "I don't think so. There's no way he committed those first three murders." They were going over old ground and would be deep into another argument if they persisted. "Look, this is gnawing at me. I can't help it. I don't mean for it to interfere with us. Why don't we put it aside? We've tried to find a key to this for three, four days. We haven't. We've been chasing it, and we haven't caught up to it. Let's relax, and let it come to us. I'm meeting Gehring again on Sunday night at Ashley's. Maybe he learned something that'll help."

Kristy put her arm through Mark's arm. "Yes, leaving it alone for a while is a good idea. Be the handsome shipwrecked brother tonight. Relax. Enjoy your Shakespeare. I will try my best to be a good Olivia. We'll fall in love during the play, we'll go home afterward and not mention a word about either Illyria, fictional or factual. Agreed?"

Mark smiled. He loved this woman. "And tonight you can tell me all about yourself. Finally."

"You want to deliver me to the world before I have made mine own occasion mellow and learned what my estate is?"

"That's very faulty Shakespeare."

"They're not my lines."

"So you intend to remain a woman of mystery?"

"Do you love me right now?"

"Yes, I do."

"So why should I change a single thing about me?"

"You are going to be the next mystery I solve."

"Shh, shh. No more talk about mysteries."

They'd reached the theatre and were soon lost in the buzz of people greeting people they hadn't seen for a few days. They snacked on sandwiches delivered by a nearby delicatessen around six o'clock and then began the serious work of getting ready to perform.

Kristy, especially, hated to play before empty seats, so five minutes before curtain, Mark checked the house and went to reassure her they had a healthy crowd to please.

She thanked him with a brief kiss, and moments later, they were in Illyria. The duke luxuriated in languid self-pity. Viola and Sebastian survived their shipwreck and found true love. Olivia and Orsino deserted their ivory towers of self-indulgence to likewise find true love. Sir Toby and his crew caused what chaos they could, while Malvolio, having received his comeuppance, stormed off, humiliated and vengeful.

Kristy as Olivia delivered her final line of the play. "He hath been most notoriously abused." Shocked, Mark heard nothing more of the little left of the play. He stood on stage stunned. The scene he'd just been a part of proved to him that Anthony Barset had had a hand in the murder of Ashley Warrington Brunner.

~ * ~

Later in Mark's apartment, as he and Kristy got into bed, he said, "I promised not to bring this up again, but…"

Kristy rolled her eyes. "I knew you had something on your mind. You've been too quiet. Now what?"

"Hear me out." Mark had one of Gehring's files with him and started leafing through it. "I have to give these back Sunday. You won't believe it—we've been acting it out for weeks now and...here, here. Read this."

Kristy took a piece of letter paper from Mark. "What is it?"

"Look at it. You tell me."

Kristy studied the paper. "It's a letter...a personal letter from Ashley to her husband."

"Husband-to-be. Check the date. They didn't get married until this deal closed, according to Gehring. Read it."

Dearest Well,

I know how hard you have been working to complete your deal with Anthony Barset. The night before I left, I heard you tell Mr. Gehring how difficult it was to come to a settlement with Mr. Barset. I could tell from what you said that Mr. Barset didn't trust you. You can imagine how that makes me feel. I haven't mentioned to you, but I've heard a few things he's said about you from friends. He's a crude but, I hope, useful man. I hope you don't disapprove, but I've written him—just yesterday, in fact—to try and convince him that you were a man he could trust, and if you told him the deal was one way and one way only, he would have to accept it. I told him we were planning to get married in a week's time, when I return (from working on my tan for you, darling), and I hoped he would see things your way and conclude this business by then. I am afraid I was angry with him for causing you so much stress—you haven't been yourself lately—and I'm afraid my anger showed up in the letter I sent him. I perhaps foolishly told him I had a number of friends willing to help you at any time, so his help might be unnecessary, and I would insist you conclude this business in the next week so we could go off on the honeymoon we planned with nothing hanging over you, nothing to take your mind away from the new life we are beginning together. Of course, you know best about this, but I hope my letter helps speed your negotiations along. I want always and only to be a help to you. I miss you and love you.

Your own Ashley

"I wonder where she wrote from," said Kristy.

"A pre-honeymoon vacation. Everyone takes one, you know. But don't you get the point?"

Kristy handed the note back to Mark. "Ashley siding with her husband-to-be? The letter's a bit groveling, and I guess she shouldn't have butted in, but..."

"Now, think of the scene Barset suggested he and Ashley play together on the island."

"Yes, I know. The final scene of the play."

"Malvolio's last scene, where he stomps off, vowing revenge. Revenge because of what?"

"He was tricked, duped by Sir Toby."

"No." Mark got out of bed and took a paperback edition of *Twelfth Night* from the dining table. He found the proper page and handed it to Kristy.

"Read the beginning of Malvolio's speech."

Kristy read:

"...Pray you peruse that letter.
You must not now deny it is your hand.
Write from it if you can, in hand or phrase,
Or say 'tis not your seal, not your invention.
You can say none of this. Well, grant it then..."

"All right. That's enough. Those would be Barset's lines. Now, Ashley, who would be portraying Olivia, says she didn't write the letter. Read Malvolio's final line as it would have been read by Barset."

Kristy skimmed down the page and onto the next. *"I'll be revenged on the whole pack of you!"* She looked up at Mark.

"It fits. Admit it. Of all the scenes to pick to play with Ashley, this is the one he chose. Didn't you think it an odd choice when he made it? And to insist he play it with Ashley?"

"Yes, I suppose I did, but I'm not following you."

Mark's shoulders slumped, and he let out a frustrated moan. "He knew he'd never have to play the scene in front of anyone, but they practiced it the morning she died. Remember, he put off running through it the day before. He waited to do the scene until the same morning he took Ashley to the marketplace. He acted out anger and vengefulness because of a letter she'd written that caused him grief."

"You're certain her letter caused Barset grief?"

"Well...no. But according to the other papers, the deal concluded five days after this letter is dated: time for the letter to get to Barset, and then a day or two later, the deal crashes down around him. *Post hoc ergo propter hoc.*"

Kristy lifted her eyebrows. "Do tell."

"Latin. The second thing happened after the first, therefore, it was caused by the first. For what other reason would Barset choose that scene?"

"Is there a copy of the actual letter Ashley wrote to Barset?"

Mark turned his palms up and shook his head. "I didn't find one, but why would it be in her husband's papers? Ashley gives us the sense of it, though, doesn't she? Ashley wrote her letter and sent it. Barset would have the sole copy."

"Suppose she didn't remember the letter. Barset couldn't make too much of it. It would have tipped her off he was angry at her. Then, when they rehearsed, if he still had the letter, he couldn't show it to her. Showing it to her would have never led to her traipsing off with him in the jeep. She'd have been wary of someone who would hold onto a letter for, what, fourteen years? She wasn't stupid. So when could he use the letter, if he had it? They weren't alone in the jeep. He dropped her off and came right back. I repeat. How could he use the letter, if it even exists?"

"It doesn't have to exist. Mentioning it would have been enough... if she recalled it."

"'If she recalled it.' Your idea breaks down a little at this point," Kristy said softly.

"It's the logical explanation for Barset's choice of scene."

"Why didn't Gehring pick up on this letter when he went through the papers?"

"Why would he? He doesn't know about the scene Barset wanted to play with Ashley. So what do you think? Another coincidence?"

Kristy shook her head slowly. "It's not quite whole yet. You're stretching—and pretty far, it seems. Remember, Barset had no opportunity to be on that cliffside with Ashley. Besides, I can't get a hold on Ashley's being pushed into space and killed in that way or for this reason."

"Someone was with her. The photo proves it. And Barset fits into this somewhere."

"All right. Don't get excited. Did you tell this to Gehring?"

"I haven't talked to him since last weekend. Anyway, it only struck me tonight. When I visit him this Sunday, I'm taking someone with me."

"Who?"

"Do you remember Moriarty?"

"Oh! Of course, I do. Are you sure he'll be necessary? I'm afraid you're going to embarrass yourself."

"I won't, and he will be necessary. I'm going to bring him in."

~ * ~

When Mark arrived outside of Ashley's apartment on Sunday evening, New York City Police Detective Walter Moriarty was in the lobby waiting for him. The detective looked as Mark remembered him—a short, chubby man around fifty, with an unruly thatch of gray hair that always seemed to be wind-tousled even in the calmest weather. He'd given up his usual black trench coat for a tan, hooded jacket with barrel buttons hooked through loops. They shook hands. They hadn't been in touch since the evening when he and Mark uncovered the murderer of Lawrence Mickelman in the basement of the Bouwerie Lane Theatre. Mark had been able to fit together the pieces of the puzzle that had perplexed Moriarty. They'd collaborated on the finish, though, and Moriarty was quite satisfied when he led the murderer out of the theatre. When Mark phoned him at his precinct desk a few days earlier, Moriarty was willing to listen.

They released each other's hand, and Moriarty said, "You promised me a murder and some good Scotch."

"That's what I promised. Let's go up."

They cleared the doorman and rode to the top floor. Gehring paused when he opened the door to two men.

"Mr. Gehring, this is Police Detective Moriarty. He and I managed to put our heads together on Lawrence's murder. I thought I needed to ask for his help now. Detective, this is Mr. Gehring, Ashley's lawyer."

"I recognize you, Detective. We spent a lot of time together for two days in a certain small room," Gehring said, shaking Moriarty's hand and leading his two guests into the living room. His reference was to the room in the police precinct where Moriarty had questioned the AWB actors after Lawrence Mickelman's murder.

"I took the liberty of promising him some good Scotch."

"Not a problem. I'll get us each a drink. How do you like yours, Detective? May I suggest you try it neat first?"

"No ice in this place?"

"I'm sure I can find some, but I'd prefer you drink this Scotch neat."

"Try it," Mark urged. "He didn't even give me an option."

"Okay, I'm game. When in Rome, be Roman, or something like that."

Soon the men took their first sips together.

"Dalwhinnie again?" asked Mark.

Gehring nodded, working his lips to extract the full flavor of the drink.

"It's...different. Good, though," said Moriarty.

"Go easy with it," Gehring advised.

"And now, Mark, you told me over the phone you were certain Barset had something to do with Ashley's murder." The lawyer lifted his bushy eyebrows to indicate it would take quite a bit to convince him.

"Let me start from the beginning so the detective knows what we do."

"Before you begin, let me tell you it's taking longer than I hoped to check on Alex Overly."

"He can wait. Let me tell my story."

When Mark finished, Gehring said, "You know, now you mention it, I remember an incident before the wedding when Wellington chastised Ashley for interfering in his business. She acted contrite and promised not to repeat her behavior. Where'd you say you found the letter?"

"A folder marked Personal Correspondence."

"Ah, that's why I missed it. I concentrated on business-related material."

"Wait a minute," said Moriarty. "Lemme see if I'm following this. This Barset guy got taken for a lot of money by Brunner, Ashley's then fiancé. She poked her nose in and told Barset to hurry up and get it over with so they could get married and live happily ever after. Now, after all this time, Barset finagles a lot Ashley's money back and, according to you, waves the whole thing in her face by acting out this scene about a letter causing trouble and finishes with a promise of revenge. Then she goes over a cliff, but he wasn't there when it happened. Guy goes to an awful lot of trouble, don't you think?"

"You don't know Mr. Barset, Detective. He is..." Gehring looked toward Mark for help.

"He is a self-indulgent, bigger-than-life blowhard who would do a thing like this because he thinks he's above it all and deserves whatever revenge he chooses to take. He gets her to sign the deal giving him the rights to her money, then she dies right after he practices that scene with her. I brought a copy of the play with me. Read this part, Detective. Won't take more than a few minutes."

"You're gonna make a freaking intellectual of me, seeing *Hamlet*, reading this. I'll give it a try."

Mark and Gehring sipped their drinks while Moriarty looked over the text. He put his finger on the page and his eyes followed the movement of his finger as he read silently. When he finished, he said, "So, he would be waving a letter at her in this scene telling her it caused all his troubles. She turns it aside, and he roars off promising revenge."

"You got it," said Mark. "What do you think?"

"And when she went over the cliff, he was back in the house?"

"Absolutely."

"You see any connection between the murder of the Brunner woman and the first bunch of murders?"

"The first three are linked but only with each other. The fourth murder doesn't fit anywhere."

Moriarty tossed the copy of *Twelfth Night* onto the red leather sofa next to him. "I don't get what it is you think you got. Nothing's connected. Your story about the letter and the acting scene..." He seesawed his right hand. "And Barset has an airtight alibi, you say?"

"That's what I say, but there could be things we don't know about, linking these events together."

"Ha, you think?" Moriarty took a sip of Scotch and looked at Mark over the rim of the glass. "I'm going to guess you already have a few things you want to try."

"I spent the last few days coming up with a thing or two, and yes, I'd like to try them. I figured I'd be on shaky ground, though, trying anything without the approval of both you and Mr. Gehring."

"I can't stop you, unless you're planning something illegal," said Moriarty.

Mark didn't respond.

"Before you start..." Moriarty put his glass to his mouth and drained it. "...we're in New York. Your murders took place a thousand miles away, a bit out of my jurisdiction."

"But if the murderer is here, in New York?"

"If the murderer is here in New York, St. Thomas would have to tell me so. They'd have to request help. They'd have to be prepared to extradite, and from what you've told me, they don't have a clue about this Barset being involved."

"Can't you talk to them?"

"Not yet, I can't. Got nothing to tell them, do I?"

"When you have something to tell them?"

Moriarty held up his empty glass. "If it's necessary. I'll let you know. Maybe tomorrow I'll make some calls and see what kind of response I get. For you." He looked Mark in the eye as Gehring rose to take both his glass and Mark's. "You were right once. If you're wrong this time, after I make a fuss about what you've told me, maybe I'm screwed."

"Look, Detective, I don't mean to cause you any grief. If what I've told you doesn't add up…"

Moriarty stopped him. He brushed back some bangs that drooped over his forehead. "Since you're batting a thousand with me, I'm willing—once—to take a chance of being screwed. My fault if it happens. Your story sounds, I'm sorry to say, unbelievable, but it'll give me something to talk to my wife about. Before I commit, though, I want to hear what you've come up with to bring this Barset fellow out into the open—and it better be good."

"Let me bring the bottle over here," said Gehring. "Keep your glasses."

"Not a bad idea," Moriarty agreed.

"I hope your other halves don't mind your coming home smelling like Scotch," Gehring said, winking at Mark.

"I told Kristy about our Dalwhinnie. She's okay."

"My wife don't give a shit one way or the other what I smell like," said Moriarty.

Gehring retrieved the bottle and put it on the coffee table. When the men had refilled their glasses, Mark began.

Thirteen

Alex Overly fancied himself a cook when it came to certain dishes, one of which he planned to prepare tonight for Barset and their Illyrian guest, Benjamin Cohen, the only one of the six investors not to buy into their island scheme. When he returned from the market with the ingredients for dinner, he noticed Barset and their guest walking on the beach, deep in conversation. He put his packages in the kitchen and went upstairs, where he knew he'd find Nelly. When he reached the top of the stairs, Nelly stepped out of her bedroom and beckoned.

"I wish you had taken me with you today," she said, closing the bedroom door behind them.

"No, no, no. I don't want Barset to have even the slightest whiff of us."

"He doesn't." She embraced him and kissed him hard.

Alex returned her kiss and moved his hands up and down along her hips. "Don't you ever wear underwear?" He stepped back.

"Remember, be discreet. Barset'll only be here for two full days with this Mr. Cohen. When they leave, we'll have everything to ourselves again."

"You don't go back with him?"

"I won't offer to go. That I can promise you."

"Good. Oh, you have a package from New York. Mr. Barset brought it over from St. Thomas."

Nelly got the package from the bed where she'd tossed it, and handed it to Alex. He looked at it—an oversized post office mailer, two-day delivery—and frowned, but said nothing.

"I will help you cook tonight," Nelly offered. "If that is not suspicious."

"It's not suspicious if we can keep our hands on the vegetables and off each other."

"It will be hard."

"What will be hard?"

Nelly laughed. "I get your silly jokes. Now go before your Mr. Barset catches you in my bedroom. Go."

Alex went to his own room at the opposite end of the hall. Once inside, he ripped open the mailer. It contained a single sheet of paper.

You should not have taken that picture of her. I will not tell what I know until I hear from you. Call 917-555-6482 at midnight any evening from the 23rd to the 27th.

Alex read the letter again. Taken what picture? And of whom? The lunatic imprisoned on St. Thomas came to mind. Obviously, the world housed more than one crazy person.

He folded the paper and thrust it into his back pocket. Why someone would spend so much on postage to send him something so meaningless? He had other things to do, like cook dinner for the two rich men waiting a floor below. He went downstairs to the kitchen to prepare for the evening ahead.

Kristy's reaction to what Mark had done shocked him. She exploded in a manner he not only had never seen from her but had never even imagined possible.

"What do you think Barset or Alex will do when they get what you sent them? You're accusing them of murder, you know." Kristy's eyes were wide and her arms waved about as if she were signaling ships at sea.

Befuddled, Mark answered the best he could. "If they don't know what the letter means, they're not guilty, and they won't do anything."

"You didn't send them letters because you think they won't know what they mean."

"Don't you want to find out who killed Ashley?"

"Don't turn this around and ask me questions like that. If you're right, they're murderers. You think they're going to call you to apologize? They may very well try to get you out of the way."

"You said they. You think it's both of them?"

Kristy screamed, "I don't think anything. They…him, what's the difference."

"Anyway, they won't know who those notes came from. I did this carefully, you know."

"Oh? How so?"

"I didn't give them my cell number or the theatre number, did I? I went out and got one of those cheap pre-paid phones to use."

"Oh, you're so brilliant, and they're so stupid. How many people could possibly have sent them a note like you did? The list is small. Oh, and let's see. Who has reputation for 'looking into things?' Who got asked to look into this? If they…he…oh, god! All they have to do is have someone call the number you gave them, be near you when the phone rings, and they know it's you."

"I won't carry it around with me. I'll keep it turned off. I only need it at midnight."

She pointed to his apartment door. "And when somebody sneaks into your hallway and stands outside to listen for the phone to ring at midnight?"

"Moriarty will be around if I need him."

"Oh, really? I don't see him. He'll be here every night at midnight?"

Mark could not meet her gaze. He didn't like looking foolish in front of this woman.

"He won't be here, no."

Kristy sat on the bed a moment but stood right away. "Mark, I don't like this. You can't take a call on that phone. It'll be too easy for them to find out who you are. And what's with the drama? Call at midnight? And why the five-day window?"

"I couldn't be certain how long it would take for the package to get to Illyria, and Barset travels a lot and might not get the mail right away. I wanted to be sure they got what I sent."

"And midnight?"

"I am trying to throw them off their game. Midnight seemed appropriate. Ominous."

Kristy refused to face him. "It's ominous, all right."

"Suggest something."

"I would like to have suggested something when my suggestion would have mattered."

Mark moved in front of her and held her by the shoulders. "It matters now."

"Barset has money."

"No argument there."

She took a step back, forcing Mark to lower his arms.

She said, "You don't know what he's capable of, who he can hire, or what gadgets he has access to that might track you down."

"He already knows where I live."

"Not you, the phone. The phone."

"Oh."

"You can't take any calls in this apartment. You can't take a call in the same place twice."

"Jesus, you've been watching too much *Homeland*. Barset doesn't work for the CIA, you know."

Kristy glared at Mark.

"All right. All right. Go on."

She paced the room for a moment, then faced him. "Be out somewhere at midnight each night. What are you going to say if someone calls?"

"They'll...he'll be calling me. All I want is to recognize a voice and hope to get some kind of admission. I plan to say someone saw him take the photograph, and we should meet. If he agrees, I'll take Moriarty to the meeting or at least him have nearby."

She turned away again. "I'm not going to stay here during this."

His heart dropped. "What do you mean?"

"I'll be in Chelsea. Call me each night when midnight passes. I need to know you're all right. And don't go to Phebe's. They might look for you there." She spun back to face him. "Promise me."

Trying to manage a conciliatory smile, he said, "I promise."

~ * ~

If he could continue his investigation on sunny, hot Illyria instead of this freezing New York City sidewalk at the dangerous and ungodly hour of midnight, he would. He'd left his apartment at eleven-thirty, honoring his pledge to Kristy. He checked his watch. Eleven-forty-five. He'd been walking along Houston Street for fifteen minutes and already the twenty-degree night had his ears singing to him. He looked up and down the street and aimed for a red glow half a block farther on.

The source of the light was a bar. Mark put his face to the window of the front door, three steps down from the sidewalk. Inside, a sodden looking, middle-aged, bearded man sat alone on a stool at the bar, toying with an empty glass. Then, the man stood up and wrestled himself into his coat. Mark's stomach clenched when the bleary-eyed man pulled the door open and stared at him. Mark tensed, ready to walk away, but the man merely mumbled something and shuffled off.

Mark looked at his watch again. It felt like he'd been out in the cold for an hour.

Eleven-fifty-eight.

More to get warm than from any desire to have a drink, he opened the bar door and walked inside. The entire place was decorated in red. He walked past red tables and chairs and pulled up a red stool to the brown wooden bar. Two red bulbs burned at each end of the bar, and red ornamental shades covered four other lamps attached to the walls.

A gray-haired bartender with a red face appeared. "What'll it be?"

Mark wondered why they hadn't hired a redhead. They could have run an ad like in "The Red-Headed League." Only red-haired men need apply. He focused his attention on the bartender.

"Always this empty?" he asked.

"At midnight on a stone-cold Monday? Yeah, I'd say so." The bartender ended his chilly statement with a chilly smile.

"I don't feel like going home yet," Mark explained.

The bartender shrugged disinterestedly. "Okay by me. I'm here till two. Drink?"

On impulse Mark queried, "Have any Dalwhinnie?"

The bartender stared at him.

"It's Scotch. Single malt Scotch."

The bartender continued to stare in what seemed to Mark weary disgust. "I know what it is. I'm a bartender, remember. You want a single malt, you grab a cab and you go north or you go south. Best I can do for you is Black Label. That suit your palate?"

"Black Label? Good. Yeah, Black Label will do fine."

The bartender rolled his eyes and turned to the tiers of bottles. While the bartender dusted off the bottle of Black Label, Mark took out his own cell phone and punched in Kristy on the speed dial. She picked up immediately.

"Kristy? Did I wake you?"

"You're joking, right. No, you didn't wake me. How can I sleep? Are you all right? Did anybody call? Where are you?"

"Sure, I'm all right. No call came, though."

"Where are you?"

"In a bar on Houston Street." He inspected his surroundings again. "A red bar. I'm going to have a drink to warm up before I head home."

"A red bar? You mean you've taken up with Communists?"

"No, I mean a bar with a lot of red lights."

"I was thinking. Why can't you have Moriarty answer the phone if it rings at midnight?"

"I explained what I planned to him, and he didn't suggest it. No one but you thinks there's any danger."

After a short silence, Kristy said, "I'm not having this conversation again. Promise me you'll have your drink and go straight home."

"I promise."

"Call me when you get there. Please. I'll wait up."

"I will."

She hung up.

His Black Label sat in front of him on the bar. The bartender had disappeared, leaving Mark alone with the wasted night, Kristy's dissatisfaction, and his drink. He tasted the Scotch. Not Dalwhinnie, but good enough. One success out of three would have to do. He sipped again.

~ * ~

The next night, a night even colder than the previous one, Mark cut the time closer. Determined to keep Kristy happy, he left his apartment and showed up at the same bar and ordered from the same bartender at eleven-fifty-four. Tonight, though, he had company.

Two people sat at opposite ends of the bar. A scraggly, gray-haired man slumped over his drink to his left, and a long-nosed woman dressed in black with shoulder-length salt-and-pepper hair sat on his right. The woman appeared the older of the two.

Mark decided not to linger. He ordered a beer to get him over the midnight threshold, and after a short call to Kristy, he'd go straight home.

He glanced at his watch. The stroke of midnight. What were Barset and Alex thinking? They must have gotten their letters by now. Why didn't they respond? He couldn't be wrong about both of them.

Suddenly, the woman laughed uproariously at something. The scraggly man had moved next to her. For some reason, her laughter depressed Mark. He looked at his watch. Twelve-ten. He'd give it five more minutes.

An occasional distant siren responding to some New York City emergency added to the dark desolation of the moment. Mark drained his beer, tucked his chin into his coat, and headed home. He'd call Kristy as he walked.

The next night, Wednesday, Mark followed the same script: a fifteen-minute walk in the numbing cold, a beer he didn't want, and a call to Kristy. At least on this night he had no scraggly or long-nosed drinking companions to depress him further.

As the week progressed with no repercussions, Mark noted a distinct improvement in Kristy's mood. He welcomed Thursday. Two more nights to go.

~ * ~

Anthony Barset returned from Illyria late on Thursday afternoon and stopped into his office. The windows faced New Jersey, and as the setting sun cast its dying orange rays across his desk, he worked his way through his mail. He wondered why Alex had been eager to stay behind on Illyria. He could have used him this coming week here in the city.

He looked up when Bertha Marder, his secretary, entered with a letter in her hand.

"This arrived while you were gone."

Barset took the envelope and studied it a moment.

"I kept it aside."

He nodded, and she left.

He opened the envelope carefully to preserve the writing on its outside. He placed the envelope on his desk and unfolded the letter. After he read it over, he reached for the telephone.

~ * ~

After Thursday evening's performance of *Twelfth Night*, Kristy asked Mark whether he wanted to give up on his idea. If he did, she promised to go home with him for the night.

Mightily tempted, he said no, he'd play out the next two nights, and a short time later had his fourth drink of the week served by Tony, the lonely bartender, with whom he was now on a first name basis, and at twelve-fifteen, he called Kristy to report, then left for his empty apartment. One more miserable night to go.

~ * ~

Early Friday afternoon, Alex Overly walked past Bertha's desk into Barset's office. He'd come straight from the airport, summoned the previous afternoon by Barset. He stayed inside for no more than thirty minutes, and when he left, he swept by Bertha without even a good-bye.

~ * ~

As Mark helped Kristy on with her coat after Friday night's performance, she made him an offer. "How about you wait for your call at Phebe's tonight? If you do, I'll come with you."

"Oh! I'd like that. I'm glad you no longer think it's dangerous."

She turned to him as she buttoned her coat. "Just because I'm willing to accompany you doesn't mean it isn't dangerous. Can you tell me why you've gotten no response?"

"No."

"I sure don't want to be with you the next time you meet Barset or Alex. They'll have figured out the letter came from you."

"Maybe. They can't be sure."

Kristy chose not to answer. Instead, she took his hand, and they left the theatre by the basement entrance. They walked the two blocks through the frigid wind and took a small table in a back corner of Phebe's. After ordering some wine and snacks, they chatted about the play as the clock moved toward midnight. When the clock hands coincided on twelve, Mark leaned toward Kristy.

"I'm sorry about this week." He pecked her cheek. "Maybe I was wrong."

"You were bold for trying." She put a finger to his cheek and leaned in to kiss his lips. The jangle of a cell phone made Mark pull back as if Kristy had set fire to his mouth.

"That's the phone!" He dug into the pocket of his coat, now dangling from the back of his chair, and pulled out his phone. "They're calling. It's them."

Kristy grasped his arm. "Let me get it. Give me. Give me. They'll be expecting a man."

Mark froze as Kristy snatched the phone from his hand and flipped it open. "I've been waiting for your call," she said, altering her voice slightly. She and Mark had watched *To Have and Have Not* the previous week, and Mark heard a touch of Lauren Bacall added to the conversation. Kristy twisted the phone away from her ear, and Mark slid his chair closer to listen.

"Are you there?" Kristy asked.

"Uh, yes. Who is this?"

Mark mouthed the word 'Alex' to Kristy.

"Not important. We need to talk. You're in trouble."

"Trouble?"

"If I want you to be. We have to talk—about a certain old woman on a certain island."

"Who is this?"

"When and where would you like to meet? You'll see who I am then."

"Where are you?"

"Would you like me to choose a spot to meet?"

"Yes."

Kristy looked at Mark, who spelled out M-E-R-A-L-S, the bar he'd spent the last four nights visiting. Kristy went her own way, though. "I'll meet you, but not until next week."

"No, no. Tonight. I'm in New York, and I can probably be where you are quickly."

Mark leaned back and shook his head at Kristy. "Tonight," he mouthed.

Kristy hit the mute button. "Let him stew," she whispered. She hit the button again. "No, next week."

"No, no. It's too far off."

"Next week."

"No, I tell you. I want to meet you right away. Tonight."

"Call me at this number next Wednesday night at six o'clock. It'll be worth your while, believe me. Wednesday at six. You call, and I'll tell you where we'll meet." She closed the phone.

Mark leaned back and threw his hands up. "Why the hell did you put him off till next week? We had him. It was Overly and in panic mode. He'd have met us tonight."

Kristy tapped his shoulder twice. "Calm down. Listen, if he's as nervous as we both heard now, imagine him in five days. He'll be paranoid waiting until next week to make the second call. We had him is right. He wasn't merely scared. He was scared to *death*. Besides, you need time to get Moriarty ready to act. And now you can send Alex the second letter you mentioned."

"Tell him we know about Ashley's letter from back when?"

"Of course. You said that was the second step."

"Yes, but only if the first step didn't work, and it did. He might not know about the letter, only Barset. Besides, he *called*, and he's ready to talk to us. If we need to, we can use the bit about the letter when we meet."

"Would you give me some woman's intuition slack? You heard his panic when I put him off. He'll be cutting out paper dolls by next Wednesday. If he gets a second letter, and he knows we've figured out what happened, he'll do whatever we ask."

Mark ran his hand through his hair. "Intuition? Oh, man. He's already ready to do what we ask. We know about Ashley's letter, but we're only supposing Barset used it like we imagine. If we make a wrong guess, he'll back off, and we'll be nowhere again."

Kristy lifted her eyebrows and said, "Hey, are you right or are you wrong about what happened? The letter, the scene, someone with her using the camera and pushing her?"

"Am I right or wrong?"

"Yes, do you or do you not believe what you've told everyone?"

Did he believe himself anymore? Yes, he did believe he had it right. "I do. It happened the way we've constructed it."

"The way *you've* constructed it, but, hey, if it doesn't work out, no problem. You're the screwup."

"What?"

Kristy laughed. "You nincompoop. This call convinced me you're right. Come on. Are you right? Yes or no?"

"I'm right. I'm right. Okay?"

"So, being right, darling, don't you think pressure should best be applied in the manner I suggest?"

Mark sighed. "I suppose. I don't know. I would have liked him here now, so we could get this over with."

"You get your second letter in the mail so he gets it in time and let him stew. Are you drinking that wine?"

"Yes, you want another one?"

"Want? I need another one."

Mark gestured to the waiter for a refill. "Should I send the second letter only to Overly or to both of them again?"

"Overly's on our hook. He said he's in New York. Send it to his office."

"You know, I'm glad you're on the side of truth, justice, and me."

"Thank you, darling. Call Moriarty tomorrow."

"I don't have to. He and Gehring and I are meeting again Sunday night at Ashley's."

"Thank you," Kristy said to the waiter who placed a glass of white wine on the table. "You'll tell them everything?"

"Of course."

"This could become dangerous soon, Mark, if it's not already."

"I'm beginning to believe you."

"Well, since you can't mail your letter until tomorrow morning, why don't we relax and enjoy the night, or what's left of it?"

"Are you staying with me tonight?"

Kristy smiled. "I am."

"Then I'll get another wine, too. You're a difficult woman to keep pace with tonight, and when we finish our wine, off home. It's been a desolate week without you."

Kristy lifted her glass, and Mark copied her with his empty glass. They clinked.

"For me, too," she said.

~ * ~

Two nights later, Mark, Detective Moriarty, and Gehring sat in Ashley's apartment, glasses of Dalwhinnie in hand.

"Does this stuff never run out?" asked Moriarty.

Gehring laughed. "All good things must come to an end, but luckily for us, Ashley bought by the case. She didn't drink Scotch, herself. She bought it for her guests. There are quite a few bottles left. Someone looked at the apartment this week, but a six-and-a-half-million-dollar apartment could stay on the market for a while in this economy. Now that you've raised the topic, though, it would be wise to take a few bottles away with us tonight—save the bother of carting it out once the apartment is sold."

"Glad to have made your acquaintance, Lawyer Gehring," said Moriarty. "Now, Mark, you said you got something to tell us."

As they drank, Mark told them everything about the phone call.

"Your girlfriend seems to have a nose for this kind of thing," said Moriarty.

"After the way she treated me during the week, she sure surprised the hell out of me. I should tell you, I put the second letter in the mail to Alex and Barset first thing Saturday. He should get it Monday."

"You don't have the actual letter you tell him about, right?" asked Moriarty.

"We only have Ashley's mention of it in her letter to her husband."

"You like to take chances."

"Watch," Mark warned the detective. "You're spilling some."

"Don't want to do that, do I?"

"No. Anyway," Mark continued, "the letter existed once. Barset must have received it. It has to be the reason for him to have chosen that specific scene to enact with Ashley. But I've already told you this."

"You're sure Alex made the call?" asked Gehring.

"Positive."

"Well, I know a little more about him than I did before. Want to hear?"

Mark and Moriarty sat back and gave Gehring the floor.

"I made calls to everyone I could think of who might have any information about him, and it seems he hooked up with Barset about fifteen years ago, a little before Barset had his dealings with Wellington. Alex tried to inject enough money to allow Barset to counter Well."

"So, he lost money, too?" asked Moriarty.

"Some. Nothing like Barset did, though."

"What about his personal life?" asked Mark.

"He's known to be something of a ladies' man. He's been married three times, always to much younger women. Didn't marry his first wife until he was forty. The wife, twenty-two. Next wife, twenty. The third, nineteen. None of the marriages lasted more than two, three years."

"Guess he doesn't like women getting old on him," said Moriarty.

"At any rate, there seems to have been no fuss at each divorce. He gives them enough money to make them happy, and they leave quietly. He lives in Dobbs Ferry."

"Awful long commute to Battery Park City," Moriarty remarked.

"True, but he and Barset sometimes rent a suite at the Waldorf— mostly when they conduct business with out-of-town guests."

"That's where they were last week when they were courting the people interested in Illyria," said Mark.

Gehring sipped his Scotch. "Barset likes to impress. So what happens next?"

Mark looked at the lawyer. "Nothing, I suppose. At least until Wednesday."

"Now you've gotten a response," said Moriarty, "I'm going to stay a lot closer to you than before. You said the call is supposed to come Wednesday at six?"

"Six, yes."

"Lemme think a minute. How about you take it in your apartment? No more of this cold beers in strange bars at midnight stuff."

"Great." Moriarty's offer would make Kristy happy, he knew.

"And you'll be sure to have some...what is this stuff?" asked Moriarty.

"Dalwhinnie," Gehring responded.

"Yeah, Dalwhinnie."

Gehring gestured at the bottle on the coffee table. "Take what you can carry. Mind if I join in on Wednesday?"

"Why not?" replied Moriarty. Turning to Mark, he said, "Kristy will have to take the call. He expects her now."

"Understood."

"We'll decide ahead of time what it is your girlfriend will say to him."

"She won't like being called my girlfriend."

Moriarty's face went momentarily blank. "Ain't that what she is?"

"Yes."

"So?"

"It's a female thing."

"Female thing?" the detective huffed. "So what should I call her?"

"Just Kristy will do."

"Kristy? Yeah, I can do that. Kristy."

"Until Wednesday, then," said Gehring, refilling his glass. "It seems we've finished with our business tonight in record time. We are finished, aren't we?"

"I suppose," said Moriarty, taking a slow sip of his Scotch. "Now you've gotten that call, though, I better get in touch with St. Thomas for sure, but not tonight,"

Mark settled back in his chair, satisfied he was finally making some progress.

Fourteen

Moriarty arrived at Mark's apartment Wednesday evening at five-thirty. He accepted Mark's offer of Dalwhinnie, saying, "Just one."

Mark refrained from joining him for the moment. He listened in on the talk Moriarty had with Kristy, and when that ended, Mark asked, "Did you make the call to St. Thomas?"

"First, I sat down with my captain. O'Banion's his name. Told him everything. Told him I wanted to work on this on my own. Told him where I'd be, what I'd be doing tonight. No problem there. I found my way to a Brian Stanhope, an officer on the St. Thomas police force. I passed along everything you told me. He gave me his polite attention, said it sounded a bit far-fetched, but promised to answer my calls and asked to be kept informed."

"He sounds underwhelmed by our story," said Kristy.

"Doesn't matter at this point. Tonight is up to us...up to you, Kristy."

"At least if we need this Stanhope, he'll have some idea of what we're talking about," said Mark.

127

Moriarty looked over the apartment. "You got a bathroom here? Indoors, I mean."

Mark laughed. "Down the dark hall."

Moriarty rose and went in search of the facilities.

The phone rang and sent a chill through Mark. "It would ring when Moriarty's in the john. Get it," Mark ordered Kristy as he got up and started after Moriarty.

"It's your cell, not the other one. Settle down." It was Gehring calling to say he wouldn't arrive until much later. Mark returned to his seat, and Kristy threw herself onto the bed, head propped on her hand, and paged through a magazine.

Mark got up from his chair and sat on the bed at her feet. "You're awfully calm."

"Not really. I'm wondering what he's going to say to me and how I should respond."

"I wonder what he's going to say, too. Do what Moriarty told you. And don't forget his power over young women. Don't let him charm you." He'd filled Kristy in about the three wives.

"He can be nowhere near as charming as you. Shoo." She waved the back of her hand at him.

Moriarty returned, and Mark went back to his chair. Across the tiny dining table, he and Moriarty chatted until, at six o'clock, the cell phone rang.

"This is it," said Moriarty. "Don't say too much. Just get him to the bar."

Kristy sat up and made the connection. "Hello?"

"Where can we meet?" came Alex Overly's voice.

"Can you be at a bar called Meral's in thirty minutes? The corner of Houston and Avenue C."

"Thirty minutes? I'll be there. I'll recognize you, won't I?"

"You will."

He hung up.

Kristy waited a moment before hanging up, too. "Not much of a conversation."

"Didn't have to be," Moriarty said. "Thirty minutes. Let's move. I don't want him there before you. And remember what I told you. Try to talk him into cooperating."

~ * ~

At six-seventeen, Kristy sat in Meral's at a small table for two in a corner to the left of the front door. Two off-duty friends Moriarty had persuaded along for the evening drank beer at the bar. At six-thirty-five, Alex Overly walked in, dressed in jeans and an olive zippered jacket. Kristy met Alex's stare and kept her eyes on him as he scanned the bar and then walked over to her.

"Kristy, I thought it might be you."

"Alex. Sit." He hung his jacket over the back of the red chair, and his white long-sleeved silk shirt looked pink in the glow of the room. The waitress approached and Kristy ordered. "I'll have a beer. Becks."

"Dewars on the rocks."

The waitress left, and Alex and Kristy looked at each other. Finally, Kristy began. "What do you have to say to me?"

"You sent me both letters?"

"I did."

"Until I heard your voice, I thought it would be your boyfriend."

"No. Me. What do you have to say to me?"

"What I have to say is I don't know what you're talking about."

Kristy's heart dropped. She hadn't expected a flat denial.

"Alex, you're here. Why did you bother coming if you don't know what I'm talking about? I found the camera. I know about Ashley's letter to Barset."

"I don't know anything about a camera."

"And Ashley's letter?"

Kristy noted Alex's hesitation. "You can't have any such letter."

"How else would I know about it?"

Alex paused again before shaking his head slowly. "You can't have any letter."

"I didn't say I had it. I said I knew about it. Where were you when Ashley died?"

"Upstairs in the house."

"No one saw you."

"So what? No one saw anything."

"Alex, I think Barset's behind this. His idea. His revenge for what Ashley's husband did to him long ago."

Small lines formed above Alex's nose, but all he said was, "If you say so. I'm only here to have a gander at you. You know, you have a lot of gall, pulling a stunt like this."

"You were frightened on the phone. Did you and Barset have time to develop a common defense? Is that what has you so cocky now?"

Alex threw his head back and drained his drink. "I'm leaving. Nothing you've said concerns me."

Kristy ignored the sweat on her palms. This had gone nothing like she'd imagined, and she couldn't let him simply leave. She had to say something, anything. The earlier conversation with Mark about young wives flashed through her mind.

"There's more. We've been talking to Nelly."

Alex's smile disappeared, but he recovered quickly.

"I have to go."

"I'd worry about being arrested soon, Alex. I'd start to think about cooperating, if I were you."

Alex stood and looked down at her. She glared defiantly up at him. At the bar, one of the drinkers pushed his stool back and got to his feet.

"It would be a stupid thing on your part to spread any rumors based on the bullshit you've confronted me with tonight. A very stupid thing." He turned and left the restaurant. One of the men at the bar trailed behind him.

A moment later, Mark came into the restaurant followed by Moriarty. He hurried over to Kristy, pulled out two chairs, and they sat. "What did he tell you?"

"Nothing. He told me nothing and denied knowing anything about Ashley's death. The camera incident is meaningless, and the letter is meaningless, or so he claims."

Mark sat up straighter. "What! And he just walked out? What else did he say? He must have said more than that."

"I did what I could. I surprised him, though, with something I mentioned at the end."

Mark leaned forward. "What?"

"I remembered about the wives and told him we'd been talking to Nelly, and his face dropped for a minute. He recovered fast, but I saw the change. I told him to worry about being arrested, and he should start cooperating."

"What did he say?"

"He warned me against spreading rumors."

"Great. We tell him what we know to be true, and he doesn't flinch. You make up something about Nelly, and he reacts."

Moriarty joined the conversation. "He took us on and came out of it, Mark."

Both Kristy and Mark started to argue with Moriarty.

Moriarty threw his hands up in mock defense. "One at a time, please."

"Go on, Kristy," said Mark.

"No, no. This is your game. I'm just frustrated. I know you're right."

"Look, Detective, he or Barset must know more about what happened on the island. Much more. Think about it—the camera, someone was with her. The letter, Barset getting back at her. I know it. And the other murders, what about them? Why did they stop with Ashley's death? And don't tell me the guy who committed them is locked up in St. Thomas. It wasn't him."

"I don't know," said Moriarty. "If Barset and Overly are involved, they've covered their tracks real good."

A startled look swept over Mark's face, and he put his hand to his forehead. "Covered their tracks. Of course! Gehring had the right idea. Can you stop Alex and bring him back?"

Kristy put her hand atop Mark's. "What are you thinking?"

He nodded toward Moriarty and didn't answer as the detective took a small gadget from his overcoat pocket and spoke into it. "Where is he?"

"Still waiting for a cab," came the crackling answer.

Moriarty responded, "Stop him. Suggest he come back into the bar."

"What's he mean?" Kristy asked Moriarty.

"Damned if I know."

She turned to Mark. "What do you mean? Gehring had the right idea about what?"

"Gehring had it figured and didn't realize it. The answer's in the Dalwhinnie."

"The Scotch he gave you?"

"The booze we drank?" Moriarty echoed. "What are you talking about?"

The police officer who had followed Alex from the bar reentered with him in tow. Alex walked over to the table.

"Hello, Alex," Mark said coldly.

Alex smiled. "A conspiracy? And who might this gentleman be?"

"I'm Detective Moriarty from the New York City Police Department."

The muscles in Alex's cheeks twitched. "I presume I may leave if I want to."

Moriarty calmly flipped one hand over. "Leave at your own risk. If I want to talk to you, I will. Convenient, like right now, or inconvenient like taking you to the precinct and sitting in a room not nearly as nice as this one." He gestured toward Kristy.

She slid over and pulled a chair from the neighboring table into the group. "Make yourself comfortable, Alex," she said.

He sat but angled his chair away from her.

"You can go after I tell you what else we know," said Mark. "You're responsible for all the deaths on the island but one, the one the lunatic committed."

Alex lifted his eyebrows in innocent surprise. "Is this more of your girlfriend's ravings?"

Mark ignored the comment. "You were going to kill Ashley in the same manner the natives had been killed, weren't you? You and Barset took turns being off the island during those first murders for an alibi. That poor lunatic copied one of your murders, got caught, and ruined your pattern. It also got you and Barset off the hook, since now you didn't have to cover for three or four murders, only one—the one you'd planned all along but hadn't yet committed. Now, though, you could hardly mimic the earlier murders. It had to be an accident. So you made it look like one. You somehow got out of the house and back into the house that day without being seen. We know someone had to be with Ashley. Someone took her picture on the spot where she fell... where she was pushed."

"Sorry. I happened to be in the house all day. No way can you prove otherwise, because that's where I was." Alex said those last words with emphasis. He stood. "Enjoy your fantasy, but please don't make me a part of it." He turned and walked toward the door. Mark leaned over to Kristy and spoke one word. "Nelly might make you a part of it," she called after him. Alex stopped a moment before continuing out the door.

"He's very nervous about something," she said. "The mention of Nelly halted him in his tracks each time. It's obvious, isn't it? You both saw."

"Can't you do something, Detective?" asked Mark.

"Nope. I don't see it. We got nothing I can use." He slumped back in his chair.

Kristy idly tapped the table a few times. "Can we go back to Mark's apartment and talk about this?"

"You asking me?" said Moriarty.

"Yes."

"Talk about it over some of that Scotch?"

"All you want."

"I'm game. You coming?" Moriarty's directed his last comment toward Mark.

Kristy pulled Mark to his feet and put her arm through his. "He's coming, Detective. He wouldn't miss it for the world."

~ * ~

Alex caught a cab to his office and brooded, holding back anger as the driver made a brisk left onto Broadway. How could they know about the letter? Right now the letter lay crumpled in a trash heap on

Illyria, if it hadn't already gone up in smoke. They *couldn't* know about it. He'd only once mentioned the letter to Nelly. He had never shown it to her. He'd tossed it into the trash first chance he got. Could Nelly have told these meddling jackasses anything?

"No, dammit, no."

"Sorry, pal?"

"No, no, nothing." Alex bent to the right as the cab caught a yellow light on West Street, turned left, and headed the final few blocks to Battery Park City. He'd have to confront her. He'd be damned if he'd keep repeating the same mistakes with these women. He almost wished he were young and starting out again—no money, chasing beautiful women at a time when he was beautiful. Barset and his moneymaking had changed everything in his life. Nelly, though, he thought he could trust. Nelly above all. How did they know about the letter? He and Barset knew. Nelly knew what little he'd told her. No one else but the three of them knew anything about it, yet these people knew.

The driver pulled to the right alongside a tiny traffic island in front of the American Express building. Alex tossed a twenty-dollar bill into the front seat.

"Keep it."

The driver gave an astonished thank you, but Alex was already out of the car.

Barset was waiting in Alex's office. Alex was afraid he would be, and there he was—sitting like a great Buddha, blowing cigar smoke toward the ceiling.

"You made it back in one piece," said Barset. "So, was it who I said?"

"Yes, Kristy, the girlfriend." Barset always gave him a monstrous bout of nerves, worse now than ever. Before he could map a clear strategy, he said, "They found out about the letter."

"The letter I gave you? Ashley's letter?"

"Yeah. The one you gave me on the island."

The thin haze of cigar smoke did little to diminish the finality in Barset's eyes. Behind him, lower New York harbor sparkled with moonlight, an occasional boat light, and the evening lights of New Jersey.

"And how did they come upon that information? And who is they?"

"I don't know how they got it. The boyfriend showed up, too."

Barset gave a small laugh. "Mark something-or-other. As I recall, I gave you the letter to show to the old bitch before you killed her. Did you?"

Alex took a breath to loosen his tongue, but his thoughts stayed frozen in his mind.

"You can't answer me." Barset took a long pull on his cigar. "This is bad. You want to tell me what the hell is going on?"

"I don't know what the hell is going on. Let's get back to Illyria and stay there. It's where our money's going. It's where our money'll be coming from soon."

Barset waved his hand before him to clear the cigar smoke. He looked at Alex and shook his head. "You always were a weak link. But, since I used your fortuitous offer of money when Brunner raped me over the Q1 deal, we've been married to each other, so to speak. Now you seem to have screwed up—royally. Somehow, because of something you did or didn't do, they are sniffing around and may soon be onto us, if they're not onto us already. Couldn't you simply have done what I told you to do? No, weak-livered, pusillanimous little dainty that you are. Well, look, I have one murder to cover up, and that crazy man did it for me. You have three."

"No one can pin Ashley's death on me. No one. There's no proof. And what covers you for the others, covers me, too."

"Think about it, friend. I dropped Ashley off and went right back to the house with Haniel. I was part of a crowd on the beach the whole afternoon. You weren't. I told them you were in your room working on papers. Guess which one of us will be a suspect?"

Alex didn't answer.

"Tell me how they found out about the letter."

"I told you...I don't know."

"Let me guess. Judy, age twenty-two. Not bad. You were forty. But then, Pearl, age twenty. You were forty-five. Heather, age nineteen. You were forty-nine. Do you notice any pattern in this?"

Alex refused to respond. He stood looking into Barset's face as he continued.

"You don't get it? Let me help you. As your age goes up, the bride's age comes down. Let me see. We have to go below nineteen." Barset drew on his cigar to give the impression of deep thought and then offered a look of mock surprise. "Nelly is eighteen. Uh-oh." Barset ostentatiously switched his cigar to his left hand and dipped his right hand into his jacket pocket.

Alex's stomach turned over and a burst of fear blasted through him.

Barset glared at him. "You have a relationship with Nelly, don't you? You talked to her. You told her things you shouldn't have, things involving me. Don't tell me. Let me guess. You're in love. She's in love...with your money, our money." He shook his head in disbelief. "You are a major albatross, and I'll be damned if I'm risking Illyria and the mountain of money it's going to bring me by being suspected of murder and God knows what else because of you."

"Let's get out of here. I have a reservation on a flight to St. Thomas tonight. You can fly down tomorrow. We'll talk. They have nothing on us. You'll see. This will die down."

"Nothing on us? There's a frightening pronoun. And who again is they?"

"I told you. Kristy and her boyfriend."

"Have they gone to the police?"

Alex's composure crumbled. "No," he lied in a soft voice.

"No? I don't believe you, Alex old friend." Barset pulled a small handgun from his pocket and leveled it at Alex. "You are history."

"You're not serious. You can't kill me. You can't. No way."

"I can and I will. It's risky, very risky, but once you're gone, and once I send Nelly back home to whatever dirty little island she crawled off of—I'm free, and I'll have everything I want out of this."

Alex glanced toward the door but didn't move. He would somehow have to talk his way out of this. He'd beg, plead, anything.

"Don't. Look, we can ride this out. No one can prove anything. Give me my share of things, and I'll disappear."

"Can you go to Illyria and slash Nelly's throat? She has to be dealt with."

"No. Of course not. They believe the lunatic did the murders. If we do another, it opens that up again."

"I thought that would be your answer. Walk downstairs ahead of me and get into my car."

"No, I'm not going with you. I have a flight booked on the nine o'clock plane."

"Do what I tell you. No one knows I'm here. To the world, I'm home alone. I left the lights on. My phone is taking my messages. The lights are on; the TV is on. I can deal with you any way I want, and no one will ever know we met tonight. Now go, Alex." He waggled the gun toward the office door.

"No." Instead, Alex moved toward the telephone.

One shot, muted and gentle, split the night, and a body fell.

Fifteen

"Don't tell me they're off the hook, Detective." Mark poured Moriarty a second, generous Dalwhinnie. They'd been talking for what seemed like hours.

Moriarty sat in the apartment's sagging, lone upholstered chair while Mark fell onto one of two wooden dining chairs.

"I'm telling you we need something more concrete," said Moriarty. "It's nothing but guesswork now."

"You know they did it. They committed all the murders except the one the lunatic did."

Moriarty shrugged. "Knowing ain't proving." They heard a knock on Mark's door. "Probably the lawyer," said Moriarty.

When Mark opened the door, Gehring hurried inside, shivering. "It must have dropped fifteen degrees in the past hour." He stood still a moment and looked at Moriarty, then at Mark. "I get the sense the evening didn't work out as planned. What happened?"

Mark took Gehring's coat and tossed it across the bottom of the bed. "Alex admitted zero, nothing," he reported. "Drink?"

"Sure." Gehring sat in the second wooden chair.

Kristy lay on her stomach across the bed.

Mark brought Gehring his Scotch. "Kristy met him, and he said he knew nothing about anything. He got up and left. The detective brought him back in, and I told him I had it figured out. He and Barset had murdered the natives to cover up their planned murder of Ashley. The lunatic fouled up their scheme when he copycatted them and got caught, so they had to make Ashley's murder seem like an accident."

"He had no reaction to that?"

"He got up and left before he could hear more," Moriarty explained. "We had to let him go. But he did react to something. Both Kristy and Mark told him the girl, Nelly, had spoken with us. That he didn't seem to like."

"Nelly? One of the live-in help?"

"The young and beautiful live-in help," said Mark.

Gehring nodded. "Yes. Overly's been susceptible to young women in the past."

"You know, I got the coverup notion from you."

"Me?"

Mark's cell rang again. "It's Don," he announced. After he brought Don up to date on the evening, he signed off and returned his thoughts to the problem at hand. "The detective insists we find something more concrete. I don't know what it would be. I thought Alex would be frightened —believe we had it figured out—and crack."

"What did you mean you got the notion from me?" Gehring repeated.

Moriarty's phone rang before Mark could answer the lawyer. "Describe him. How long ago? Who's there? I'm on my way." Moriarty ended the call. "There's been a shooting. Cleaning lady found a body in your friend Alex Overly's office."

"Who's been shot? Alex?" asked Mark.

"No identification on the body, but I got a description. Large and overweight. Fifty-five, sixty years old."

"That's not Alex," said Mark.

"Sounds like Barset," said Kristy.

"Barset? How could it be Barset?" asked Mark. "You said Alex's office?"

"So the cleaning lady tells us."

"If it's Barset's body," said Gehring, "I wonder if it's because of something that happened with Alex tonight."

"Let's get over there and see what we can find out," said Moriarty.

"All of us?" asked Kristy.

"Why not? We're a team, ain't we?"

They grabbed their coats and sped toward Battery Park City in Moriarty's unmarked car.

~ * ~

Mark stared at the body sprawled behind the desk. "It's Anthony Barset," he said to Lieutenant Baxter, the officer in charge at the moment. Baxter wrote the name down.

"Anything happen I don't know about yet?" Moriarty asked the lieutenant.

"Right after we got here, a car service phoned Overly's office looking for him. His ride to the Delta terminal at Kennedy was downstairs waiting. We sent somebody down to the car, but Overly never showed."

"Kennedy," Mark repeated. "He must be going to Illyria."

"Why didn't he take the limo?" asked Kristy.

"Because of this." Mark pointed at Barset's body. "He couldn't wait around, so he grabbed a cab and bolted."

Mark pulled out his cell phone. "I'll look up the number for Delta Airlines." He punched in some numbers. "Yes, I'm looking for a flight to St. Thomas. Do you have a flight tonight leaving from Kennedy Airport? What time's it get into St. Thomas? Thanks." He looked up at his audience. "Leaves at nine o'clock with a thirty-minute layover in Atlanta."

Moriarty checked his watch. "Three minutes from now. Get the number for Kennedy Airport."

Mark found it on his cell and handed the phone over to Moriarty.

"Give me airport security," he barked. "Listen, this is Detective Walter Moriarty, New York City police. There's someone I want taken off the Delta plane to St. Thomas that's about to leave. What do you mean it left? Aren't you guys famous for your delays? Delta. Doesn't ever leave the airport, you know? All right. All right. Good-bye." He faced the others. "You heard. He's gone."

"Now what?" asked Mark.

Kristy offered a suggestion. "Why not call the fellow you talked to on St. Thomas. Stanhope, right? Alex murdered people under their jurisdiction. Stanhope can at least hold him for you, and..."

"Wait," cried Mark. He searched on his cell phone again. "We took American Airlines non-stop when we flew down there. I've got the number." A moment later he said, "Yes, American Airlines. I'd like to book a couple of seats to St. Thomas tonight. Any available?" He listened. "It's a direct flight, right?" He stared at Moriarty. "You have two seats? Good. What time's it get in? Great." He answered the ticket clerk's questions and provided his credit card number. "I'll be able to pick up the tickets at the gate, right? Good! Don't worry, we'll make it."

When he ended the call, he said, "Detective, you and I have two seats to St. Thomas. It leaves at nine-forty but gets in a little before Overly's flight. We can be there to meet him."

"Ain't that another country?" asked Moriarty. "I don't have my passport in my pocket, you know."

"You don't need one," said Mark. "It's a U.S. territory. We didn't have them when we went the first time. You get in touch with your man on St. Thomas and have him get a warrant for Overly, or at least alert him that you want him held until we can sort things out. We don't want him to get to Illyria. You know, this has a chance of working out. It does. But we have to get to JFK in about thirty-five minutes."

"My wife's gonna have a coronary she hears I'm off to the islands without her," said Moriarty. Nonetheless, he had an officer rush Mark and him to the airport, sirens and lights at full bore. Flashing his badge at every opportunity, Moriarty got them to the plane with four minutes to spare.

~ * ~

The first thing Mark did on reaching the airport at St. Thomas was check the TV monitor displaying the status of incoming flights.

"Overly's plane is on time and ten minutes out, Detective."

"Listen," said Moriarty, "you keep Overly in sight when he gets off the plane."

"Where are you going?"

"I gotta find Stanhope. He better freakin' be here. And don't let your friend get right on another plane and fly off."

"I won't. If he looks like he's leaving right away, I'll call you. I'll go to Gate Two and wait for him. You go do what you have to."

Moriarty hurried away, and Mark scanned the walls, found Gate Two indicated, and headed off.

He ducked inside a small shop—sundries and snacks—nearby and looked over the terminal. A few travelers lingered in the waiting area. Mark yawned and stretched. It had been a long, long day, with the end not yet in sight. He looked over the magazines and kept an eye on the gate. A few minutes later, people began to pass through the gate and enter the terminal.

Alex entered, paused, and looked back, as if expecting someone to join him. Then Nelly came through the door and attached herself to Alex's arm, laughing.

A bar, dimly lit and, at this time of night, sad looking, was open and Alex and Nelly, lugging their carry-on bags, went straight for it. Mark left the sundries shop and trailed behind them. Alex and Nelly chose a table in the bar and sat. Mark looked around for Carlos. No Carlos meant no airplane.

Through the bar's window, Mark watched Alex go to the bar and return with two bottles of beer and two glasses. He sat, poured, and began talking with Nelly.

Mark stepped back around the corner out of sight. What was Nelly doing getting off the same plane as Alex? She'd been in New York with Alex, unnoticed and unmentioned? If Alex returned to New York because of the letter, why would he lug Nelly along? Alex's reaction to the comments about Nelly came back to him.

Mark checked on the pair again through the window. They still sat, talking and drinking in high spirits. He turned aside, took out his cell phone, and called Moriarty. "Did you find Stanhope? They're having beers in the airport bar."

"Stanhope's waiting for two officers to come with us. And who is they?"

"Alex and, surprise, Nelly."

"Nelly? The young woman from the island? Did she meet him?"

"No, she flew with him."

"Really? What do you make of that?"

"I don't know." Mark glanced through the window again. "How long before you get here? We miss them, be hard to get them back."

"Won't be long. Stanhope's talking to two officers right now. I'll be out of here in a minute. Don't worry, we won't miss them."

"Come right to the bar in the terminal and let me take the lead. When I tell you to take the girl out of there, do it fast. Hear me? Fast."

"You're directing again, eh?" Moriarty said with a chuckle, referring to Mark's planning out the unmasking of Lawrence's murdered in the basement of the theatre on the opening night of *Hamlet*. "I'll tell Stanhope. Let me get back to him."

Mark returned to his post and noticed Alex check his watch, then rise and walk to the far side of the bar, where a series of large picture windows faced the dark runways. Alex put his hand to his brow and looked left and right through the window.

Mark knew he was searching for Carlos and the plane from Illyria, a fifteen-minute flight away. He hurriedly scanned the terminal in vain for Moriarty.

When Alex returned to his table, he lifted his glass and motioned toward Nelly with it. After draining her drink, she beamed a bright smile Alex's way.

A hand touched Mark's shoulder and he jumped. "Damn, you startled me."

Moriarty moved his group a few steps around the corner from the bar.

Stanhope was a small, clean-shaven man on the near side of forty with neatly combed straw-colored hair dressed in casual clothes. "Pleased to meet you. Astonishing your story proved true. Quite a bit of insight on your part, Mr. Louis." Two burly uniformed officers stood behind Stanhope.

"Thanks. You tell him what I said to do?" Mark asked Moriarty.

"I told him."

"You want the female out quick, right?" said Stanhope.

"As soon as I say so."

"No problem."

"They still there?" asked Moriarty.

"Yeah, their plane to Illyria hasn't shown up yet. Shall we?" Mark led them back around the corner and entered the bar.

Alex had risen and was pulling Nelly's chair back. He froze when he saw Mark and Moriarty coming toward him.

"Alex, it's over," said Mark. "We know almost everything."

Stanhope stepped forward, flashing a badge. "You'll have to come with us, Mr. Overly."

"Nelly," Mark went on, "you were great. You gave us everything we needed to know, and with Barset's murder, we have more than enough to arrest Alex. We have you for two murders, Alex. Ashley's and Barset's. Thanks, Nelly. Have her taken to your office, Officer Stanhope, while we attend to Alex."

One of the uniformed officers took Nelly's arm and moved her away. Nelly gave Alex a stunned look over her shoulder.

"Detective, you can take Alex into custody now," said Mark.

Moriarty produced handcuffs. "Hands behind you."

"Where's she going?" Overly asked, his eyes trailing after Nelly.

Nelly and the officer had already disappeared from the bar. Mark answered, "She gave us everything we need, Alex. We talked to her a few times in Illyria. She called when she found out she was coming to New York and decided to help us out with the whole story, reluctantly at first, but when she learned the consequences of not helping, she changed her mind."

Mark hoped Moriarty would catch on, and the detective did not disappoint.

"That's right," added Moriarty. "She's smart. Accessory to murder can carry as much time in the lock-up as murder can. Her testimony will go a long way to keeping her out of jail, though."

"Wait, wait, wait," Alex pleaded.

Moriarty had pulled Alex's arms behind him and locked the handcuffs into place. Alex pulled free of Moriarty.

"Where is she going?" Alex asked again.

"Home," answered Mark. "Back to Illyria until we need her."

"Don't worry," said Moriarty. "You'll bump into her again...at your trial."

"She's going home? Back to Illyria?"

"Back to Illyria," Mark repeated. "Carlos will fly her home when he gets here."

"No, no. She said she never spoke to you. She said she didn't tell you about the letter. I talked to her on the plane. She swore..."

Moriarty took Alex's arm. "What do you think she's going to tell you, pal? Let's go."

"But she told me...She's going back to the island?"

"Alex, it's over," said Mark. "We know everything. She's the one who told us how you planned to cover Ashley's murder with the other ones. Rest assured, we know. Go with the detective and don't make a scene."

"You'd better do as he says," said Stanhope.

Moriarty led Alex a few steps toward the bar entrance, but Alex pulled away again. "Accessory? No, no. She's not my accessory. I'm hers. Let *me* talk to you and stay out of prison. You got it backward, my friend."

Mark tried to hide his bewilderment. "What are you saying, Alex?" he asked.

"She's not my accomplice at anything. You're wrong. It's the other way around. She's lying. Believe me, she's lying to save herself at my expense. No, sir. I'm not having that happen."

"Alex," said Moriarty. "Who killed Ashley? Who killed Barset?"

"Not me. Nelly left the house that day. She killed the old lady. I was upstairs. She left the house. Nobody paid any attention to her. She's a servant. She pushed Ashley onto the rocks. And Barset was two seconds away from killing me when she shot him."

"Why would she kill Ashley?" Mark asked, a wave of anger cresting inside him. "Why, Alex?"

Alex didn't answer. The burst of righteous indignation that led him to proclaim his innocence wilted before Mark's question.

"Let's go to the security office," said Moriarty. "We need to have a long talk with you, buddy."

This time when Moriarty took Alex's arm, he made no protest. Head down, Alex allowed Moriarty to set the pace. Stanhope and the uniformed officer bracketed them. Mark stared at Alex's back a moment before following along.

~ * ~

After conversations of some length with both Alex and Nelly, Mark somehow found the energy to get back on a plane early the next morning while Moriarty stayed to work things out with Stanhope. He slept on the plane and slept again for another few hours at home before summoning up the will to perform on the stage of the Bouwerie Lane Theatre.

Much to the annoyance of his friends, and after an apology to Kristy, he went straight home alone after the play, claiming a need for some sleep. Moriarty called him from St. Thomas the next day, Friday, and brought him up to date. Don, Kristy, Karen, and even Gehring called right after he got off the phone with Moriarty, and he promised each of them to tell the whole story in Phebe's after the evening's play ended.

A little past eleven, they gathered around a table.

Gehring spoke first. "We've heard about Nelly killing Ashley and Barset, but precious little else. It's going to take a bit of explaining to get from your company's invitation to Illyria to Nelly pushing Ashley off that cliff."

They'd ordered food and were working on their first round of drinks as they waited.

"Well, here goes," said Mark. "Our initial guesses were pretty good. Barset believed Ashley's husband swindled him. He felt Brunner's tactics went far beyond even the cutthroat tactics he came to use himself. When Ashley wrote her letter, it rubbed Barset the wrong way, to say the least. According to Alex, he believed what Ashley wrote in her letter and thought she somehow brought money to the deal that helped put it over for her husband."

"That never happened," said Gehring. "Ashley was an actress back then, as lacking in funds as most actors."

The four actors looked at Gehring.

"No offense."

Mark continued. "Barset had it in his mind, nonetheless, that Ashley had tipped the scales against him. When he met up with her again and knew she had her deceased husband's millions at her disposal, he began to plan. He seems to have had such a hold over Alex, financial and otherwise, that he drew Alex in, whether he liked it or not."

"And the one blurry photograph got you on the track?" Gehring asked with some awe. "Extraordinary."

"The photo plus the other stuff. No dirt on Ashley's clothes or her fingernails. The illogic of the squatters' murders. I remembered Barset suggesting Ashley go and walk around the marketplace the final day. Alex's manner after the murder. Too many things were going on under the surface. Barset's and Ashley's histories we discovered together. You know about the letters we sent and Alex showing up. Bit by bit it added up."

"Who killed the first three squatters on the island?" asked Don. "More wine anyone?" Don refilled the necessary glasses as Mark explained.

"Barset wanted Alex to do the dirty work. He planned for Alex to kill a couple of natives, three of them, and then kill Ashley in the same manner after Barset had secured as much of her money for his project as he could. Ashley's death would have been part of the pattern. Not much of an investigation could be mounted on the island. Alex, though, couldn't make himself kill a native, until Barset forced him to. Barset, himself, committed the first murder to shame or goad Alex into the next two—sort of a see-how-easy-it-is example."

"Barset murdered the first native?" Gehring asked in disbelief.

"He did," said Mark. "That forced Alex to commit the next two murders, and Ashley would have been the fourth. But the lunatic killed a native and got himself caught. It threw their whole scheme upside down. Now Ashley's death had to look like an accident."

"Why didn't they plan to make Ashley's death look like an accident in the first place?" asked Kristy, breaking off a piece of bread from the basket on the table. "Why kill those poor natives?"

"Alex said they couldn't be sure Ashley would put herself into a position where an accident would be plausible. They couldn't be certain she would stand alone on a rocky precipice. As a matter of fact, Alex insists he argued with Barset over the need to murder those natives, since he knew he would be the one who had to do the killing."

"And at first he couldn't do it?" asked Don. "Thanks." He took the proffered bread basket from Kristy.

"So he says. Not until Barset shamed him into it."

"And Ashley?" Gehring prodded.

"Alex's responsibility, but after meeting her, talking to her... he says he couldn't do it, especially after having already killed two people. As it happened, he and Nelly were a hot item. He promised to marry her, and he confided Barset's plan to her. The promises of marriage, riches, Illyria, enabled Alex to convince her to commit the act he couldn't bring himself to do.

"Alex was in his room the last day as he claimed, but hiding from Barset. Barset thought he'd gone out to do his chore. Nelly slipped out unnoticed—we were on the beach, Barset included. She met Ashley 'by accident' in the marketplace, showed her around, and took her photograph."

"And pushed her," Gehring concluded. "Unbelievable."

Mark broke the momentary silence at the table. "Barset saved the original letter Ashley wrote to him and gave it to Alex. He was supposed to show it to her before he killed her and remind her of the scene she'd practiced earlier with Barset. Barset ordered Alex to rub it in real good. Alex had no stomach for the drama involved and threw the letter away, but only after, fortunately for us, telling Nelly about it. It prevented his being certain Nelly didn't tell us about the letter."

"Better to be lucky than good," said Don.

"Mark was both," Kristy said, reaching over and stroking Mark's arm.

Mark gave Kristy's palm a quick kiss. "No, no, we have you to thank, my quick-thinking darling, for having Alex wonder about Nelly turning against him."

"I knew I had to do something when Alex didn't appear threatened and got up to go. I panicked."

Don cleared his throat. "And that should learn us *There's a divinity that shapes our ends, Rough-hew them how we will.* Shakespeare comes through again."

Kristy shrugged. "What can I say? I remembered you telling me about Alex's predilection for younger women, so I said Nelly's name, and he reacted to it. I told Mark he reacted. Mark made me repeat Nelly's name to him when he left the restaurant the second time, and he reacted again."

Mark toyed with his empty wineglass. "Then, who do we find accompanying him on the plane from Illyria but Nelly! She'd been with him in New York, so it would have been easy for Alex to imagine her getting in touch with us. We were a phone call away. She waited in his office the night he met us and hid in the next room when Barset showed up to wait for Alex. Alex claims that when Barset took out a pistol, he was certain Barset was going to shoot him, but Nelly stepped into the room and shot Barset. Alex took both pistols with him and tossed them in a trash can at the airport."

"How'd she happen to have a gun?" asked Don.

"Alex was afraid of Barset, afraid of what Barset would do if he knew he had Nelly with him. Alex kept a small pistol in his desk, and he showed it to Nelly, I guess to demonstrate the level of his fear. When she heard Barset coming into Alex's office, she took the gun and slipped into the conference room to listen to their conversation.

Barset insisted Alex go back to Illyria and kill Nelly, and, uh, she knew what to do about that and saved Alex's life at the same time."

Gehring idly unfolded his napkin and put it on his lap. "And what will happen to Alex and Nelly?"

"Moriarty and Stanhope are still trying to sort out who gets tried where and for what. They've got five murders and accessories to murder to sort out."

"So Detective Moriarty's still in St. Thomas?" asked Gehring.

"Still in St. Thomas. I spoke to him this morning."

Kristy sighed. "Nice work if you can get it."

Gehring raised an index finger. "I have one more question. In your apartment the night you met Alex, you said I gave you a clue that cleared things up, and I can't for the life of me figure out what it might have been. I don't have a clue, if you will."

Mark laughed. "Your story of how you tried to hide your Dalwhinnie from your wife. You covered up the earlier drinking by having a drink as soon as you got home. Alex and Barset did the opposite. They wanted to cover up the last murder by committing a series of earlier murders."

"Ah, I see. Pretty sporting of me to let you figure it out and take the credit, wasn't it?"

Mark smiled. "I appreciate your restraint."

"What happens to Ashley's money now?" asked Don. "I have a reason for asking."

They looked to Gehring for an answer. "I can tell you where it won't go—Barset Enterprises. I expect it will get divided somehow among the current beneficiaries."

"We're one of them, right?" asked Mark.

"It appears so. The court will not likely have come upon a will like this...maybe ever...with so many beneficiaries. Sorry, I have no definitive answer for you. I assure you, though, whatever can be done for the AWB Theatre Company, I will do."

Mark turned to Don. "And your reason for asking?"

"I'm off to Hollywood, and I want to leave you in good shape when I go." A broad smile spread across Don's face.

"You got the part!" cried Kristy.

"I did. I got a call this morning. I told Karen. Now I'm telling you."

"When do you go?" asked Mark.

"At the end of our run of *Twelfth Night*. They don't start shooting for two months. It gives me time to get a place to live and settle in."

"Well, I guess that makes it a happy ending all around. Congratulations." Mark lifted his glass toward Don, and everyone followed suit as the night of celebration wore on.

~ * ~

Kristy and Mark, bundled up against the cold, walked along Houston Street toward Mark's apartment.

"You did well," said Kristy. "You're everyone's hero, and thank goodness I haven't heard any 'Enough, no more. 'Tis not so sweet as it was before.'"

"Did I say that?"

"I recall you did."

"Drama king. Well, I've been kept busy."

Kristy briefly wrapped both her arms around Mark's left arm as they walked. "So you know what it takes then."

"I should depend on different friends being murdered to keep me from getting depressed?"

"Keeping busy does not, we'll hope, mean depending on the kindness of murderers. The theatre should keep you plenty busy now. I want to help out with what you're doing with the theatre, you know."

"That would be welcome. I always anticipate with glee you working under me."

Kristy bumped him with her shoulder. "Cute."

"But, you know, I missed a couple of things early on in this case. May I call it a case? I feel like Basil Rathbone when I say 'case.'"

"You may call it a case."

"Thanks. Aren't you interested in knowing what I missed?"

"I am. Tell me inside."

They climbed the stairs of Mark's building and entered the apartment. Mark took both coats and hung them in the closet. He threw himself on the bed and watched Kristy take off her clothes.

When she threw on an oversized AWB T-shirt, he moved over and gave her room on the bed. She lay on her stomach and looked at him. "You missed?"

"Gehring spoke of two nasty weeks of negotiations. Ashley wrote her letter during that time. Two weeks was a general period of time. It was the twelfth night of this stretch that the deal fell away from Barset. Twelfth night—*Twelfth Night*. Get it?"

Kristy stared at him. "You're telling me knowing that would have made a difference?"

"Alex mentioned it. He said Barset laughed about it."

She shook her head. "No normal person, not even a super sleuth, would have thought of that. Not Basil Rathbone, not Jeremy Brett, not even that Cumberbatch fellow."

"Who?"

"BBC. We watched it. Never mind. Go on."

"Maybe you'll like the second one better."

"I'll have to."

Mark rose and undressed. "Guess when Barset first extended his invitation to Ashley to visit Illyria."

"Don't know. After Christmas sometime?"

"January sixth."

"January sixth. So?"

"January sixth happens to be Twelfth Night, the official Twelfth Night of Christmas."

Kristy sighed. "You were supposed to recognize that as a clue, too?"

"It was there."

"Come here."

Mark returned to bed and cuddled next to Kristy.

She put her arms around him and put her lips next to his ear. "Here's another clue, Basil. You want to know about me? Suppose I told you I've had eleven other lovers, all wonderful men, true knights in shining armor. Do you know what that would make you?"

"Jealous?" said Mark.

Kristy turned off the lamp next to the bed, the one light burning in the room. "No, silly. It would make you my Twelfth Knight."

Mark frowned and pulled back to ask a question, but Kristy wouldn't allow it. She threw herself on top of him, giggling madly.

"No more talk," she whispered and kissed him hard. The room grew quiet.

Meet John Paulits

John Paulits lives in New York City and spent many years there teaching. He has written fiction for over forty years, novels for children as well as adults. *A Dying Fall* is his fourteenth book for Wings ePress. To learn more about John's books, visit him at: www.johnpaulits.com.

Other Works From The Pen Of

John Paulits

For ages 8-12

Philip Gets Even - By accident at an art show in which they are entered, Philip Felton and Emery Wyatt offend Johnny Visco, the toughest boy in sixth grade, and he promises to get even. When Johnny Visco's attacks show no sign of stopping, Philip, Emery, and Mr. Conway concoct a plan that finally puts Johnny Visco in his place and prevents him from tormenting the boys any longer.

Philip and the Case of Mistaken Identity - Philip and his best friend Emery, detectives on the trail, try to cope with a mystifying little girl who runs them a merry chase.

The Director - The Director invites nine-year-old Tommy Whitaker to be a character in a book set in 1957. The trouble begins in the Regal movie theatre, where after the Saturday matinee. Elwood Wambo, the strange caretaker of the movie theatre, hires Tommy and his 1957 best friend, Mouse, to stay behind on future Saturdays to clean the theatre when the movie is over. The boys later learn that Wambo and his partner Jeremy are part of a gang of thieves. When their friend Smitty's bike is stolen and when Smitty himself mysteriously disappears, Tommy and his two friends, Mouse and Royal, vow to solve the mysteries of their missing friend, his missing bike...and a murder.

A Cat Tale - Hayden and his fellow cats find their way to paradise: Talula Tupperman's Home for Distressed Felines. But

Rodney and Stanley, cat kidnappers, are on their trail, and suddenly cats begin to vanish. Can Hayden and his troop put a stop to these mysterious disappearances before they mysteriously vanish, too?

The Mountaintop - Jason, a seventeen-year-old Amerian, sets out for the mountaintop to determine the truth of his people's beliefs. On his journey he runs into some unexpected and eye-opening adventures. Most importantly, he meets Manda, a 17-year-old Ginder girl, who changes his life irrevocably.

For adults

Hobson's Planet - When Culp Robinson arrives on the Hobson's Planet, he steps into a whirlwind of controversy and political upheaval. Against his will, Culp finds himself the designated savior to another planet. Having failed on Earth, he wants no part of another such quest. Now he must decide where his duty and his heart lie.

Henny and Lloyd Private Eyes - Henny and Lloyd, age mid-twenties, have completed their online course in private detecting and are now licensed PIs. They've rented an office on Centre Street in downtown NYC, a rundown apartment each in Williamsburg, Brooklyn, and now set out to make their dreams of crime-fighting come true.

Ant-Nee's Golden Notebook - Mayhem and mix-ups follow Bruno Brunotaglia's murder of a hit man sent after him by a rival mob. Panic stricken, Bruno leaves behind a briefcase of money and an import notebook. Two down-and-out friends find the briefcase and notebook, and Bruno needs them back before his father, head of the Philly mob, blows a gasket. Will Richard get to keep the briefcase of money he found with Strangler and the Indian hard on his trail? Can Clarence make hay from the information in the notebook? It's a battle of half-wits in this deadly game of hide and seek.

The Sad Case of Brownie Terwilliger - Brownie Terwilliger looks at his opportunity of running for mayor of Philadelphia as a chance to right the wrongs of a city. He hopes to oust Milton Streezo, the incumbent, but Streezo does not take kindly to this challenge and concocts a plan to destroy Brownie, even hiring Lunky Ledbetter, famed perpetrator of dirty political tricks. Can Brownie withstand the onslaught? Will he have the opportunity to do some good in the world? Don't bet on it.

The Collected Short Stories - A man buried alive; the extinction of a gloried species; the mingling of interstellar races; a mysterious amulet; a fearful child; an animal-loving old hag; the assassination of the Almighty. Stories of horror, mystery, fantasy, and science fiction certain to raise the hairs on your neck.

The Rest is Silence – The Shakespeare Murders, Vol 1
When a body is found on the stage of the Bouwerie Lane Theatre, the AWB Theatre is thrown into turmoil, and Don Lovett, one of its actors, is suspected of murder. Can AWB actor Mark Louis exonerate his good friend and bring the life of the acting troupe back to normal?

Writing as Paul Johns:

From Out the Shadowed Night - How far would you go to achieve revenge? Brian Martin committed an unspeakable crime and managed to escape responsibility for his act. Now, sixteen years later, not only do the effects of his crime rise up out of the past, but something much more deadly begins to haunt him as well.

Prayer Preyer - Fifty years of obstacles have kept Jerry Curtis from locating Father Lockhart. Now, he's found the priest and is determined to take his revenge for the crime committed against him all those years ago.

Letter to Our Readers

Enjoy this book?

You can make a difference.

As an independent publisher, Wings ePress, Inc. does not have the financial clout of the large New York publishers. We can't afford large magazine spreads or subway posters to tell people about our quality books.

But we do have something much more effective and powerful than ads. We have a large base of loyal readers.

Honest reviews help bring the attention of new readers to our books.

If you enjoyed this book, we would appreciate it if you would spend a few minutes posting a review on the site where you purchased this book or on the Wings ePress, Inc. webpages at: https://wingsepress.com/

Thank You

Visit Our Website

For The Full Inventory
Of Quality Books:

Wings ePress.Inc
https://wingsepress.com/

Quality trade paperbacks and downloads
in multiple formats,
in genres ranging from light romantic comedy
to general fiction and horror.
Wings has something for every reader's taste.
Visit the website, then bookmark it.
We add new titles each month!

Wings ePress Inc.
3000 N. Rock Road
Newton, KS 67114